The Mayor of Castlebridge

The Mayor of Castlebridge

❀

An Irish Adaptation of a
Thomas Hardy Classic

Ronan Scanlan

iUniverse, Inc.
New York Lincoln Shanghai

The Mayor of Castlebridge
An Irish Adaptation of a Thomas Hardy Classic

Copyright © 2005 by Ronan Scanlan

All rights reserved. No part of this book may be used or reproduced by any means, graphic, electronic, or mechanical, including photocopying, recording, taping or by any information storage retrieval system without the written permission of the publisher except in the case of brief quotations embodied in critical articles and reviews.

iUniverse books may be ordered through booksellers or by contacting:

iUniverse
2021 Pine Lake Road, Suite 100
Lincoln, NE 68512
www.iuniverse.com
1-800-Authors (1-800-288-4677)

The characters portrayed in this story are fictional. Any perceived resemblance between them and any real person, either living or dead, is purely coincidental.

ISBN: 0-595-34414-3

Printed in the United States of America

To

Megan Leanne Wickham

Contents

❀

Chapter 1   A Done Deal... 1
Chapter 2   First Regrets 10
Chapter 3   Eighteen Years Later 15
Chapter 4   Of Mills and Grown Barley....................... 21
Chapter 5   Supper at The Pikeman's Inn 29
Chapter 6   Family Matters... 34
Chapter 7   Sound Advice... 43
Chapter 8   Trouble at Mill... 49
Chapter 9   The Truth Revealed 55
Chapter 10 Too Close to Call 66
Chapter 11 A Grand Day Out....................................... 74
Chapter 12 The Choices of Lucy Devereux................. 81
Chapter 13 Rash Dealings... 93
Chapter 14 A Couple of Days Off............................... 105
Chapter 15 A Reversal of Fortunes............................ 111
Chapter 16 Echoes from the Past 121
Chapter 17 Dusty and Krusty..................................... 126
Chapter 18 The Longest Day 132
Chapter 19 A Knock at the Door 139
Chapter 20 The Sand Dunes of Curracloe................. 144
Chapter 21 The Departure of Michael Hendrick 151

Acknowledgements

Sincere gratitude is due to several individuals for their invaluable advice and assistance during the compilation of this book. My storyline proofreaders—Keith Pinkerton and His Honour Judge Peter Smithwick, an historian—are both commended for their unrivalled attention to detail. I'm further obliged to my dear sister Eileen for her cover picture and also to my mother, a native of Enniscorthy, for her indispensable advice on the subtleties of the Wexford dialect.

I'm also greatly indebted to James O'Brien, whose vast knowledge of 19th century coins and banknotes served to enhance the historical authenticity of the narrative. Thanks also to Elaine Ferguson for her reliable, detailed and accurate information regarding County Wexford's ecclesiastical history. What's more, informative interviews with a number of local Castlebridge residents greatly lessened my ignorance of their town's history. I am especially grateful to local clergy and local businessmen—in particular Liam Keating—for their time and interest.

Too numerous to name are the several other friends, colleagues and family members who offered their support, encouragement and interest in the novel from composition through to publication. The greatest tribute of all, however, is due to the finest tragic author of the 19th century—Thomas Hardy. It was Hardy's classic novel 'The Mayor of Casterbridge', coupled with a realisation of the eerily striking similarities between Castlebridge and Dorchester (Casterbridge), that inspired this adaptation.

Finally, heartfelt thanks are due to Betty Cortus and her colleagues at the Thomas Hardy Association for their greatly informative research, kindly undertaken, regarding copyright expiry dates on the plot.

CHAPTER 1

❀

A Done Deal

Wellingtonbridge had no grandeur. Wellingtonbridge had no pretences. Wellingtonbridge had no particular prominence among the rural villages of County Wexford in those early decades of the nineteenth century. Sixteen uneventful years had passed since the turmoil of 1798. Through a round dozen of months the good folk of Wellingtonbridge had tilled, ploughed, sowed, laboured and traded with as much routine as any similar town-land in the Wexford of that particular epoch. But through five busy days, at the outset of each harvest season, the village assumed an importance so manifestly out of proportion to its size and influence, as to render the scene almost absurd. For each autumn was held, without fail, the great Wellingtonbridge Fair.

One particular autumn evening, as that same fair was drawing to its close, a young couple could be observed striding towards the village from its western road. The man was cloaked and booted as if for a journey of some leagues, nor did his appearance just then suggest that any such distances would tire him or wear him down. For he was of considerable frame, and his stride a stately one. Indeed, his advance along the dust trail leading to the village was in a manner and of a pace so deliberate that his female companion frequently lagged behind, often requiring her to upgrade her own pace to a gentle trot. Notwithstanding these frequent attempts to maintain a degree of physical proximity to her husband, the woman journeyed alone. She was alone because the man to whom she was bound in marriage could hardly have been any less attentive to her. For Susanna Hendrick the day's journey was, to all intents and purposes, a solitary one.

Her aloneness and solitude were relieved, or at least mitigated, by the sudden but not untimely awakening of the young child she'd borne in her arms for several hours. Although this couple had clearly traversed great distances that very afternoon, a casual observer on the outskirts of Wellingtonbridge might have been forgiven for supposing that the company's opening exchange of the day was comprised of the half-insensible utterances of the year-old child and her mother's half-interested replies. But any interchange between members of this peculiar travelling party was to be welcomed, as it lent to them an air of humanity hitherto greatly lacking in their fellowship.

Thus, as they walked, the village of Wellingtonbridge lay before them. That the season for gathering had arrived there could be little doubt. Even as the Hendrick trio entered the village from its western side, vivid reminders surrounded them that this most important of seasons was upon one and all. As it cast their shadows so precisely before them, the westering sun now glowed with that intense tangerine richness so peculiar to the close of a bright autumn day. Thus, as the small family group raised their glances from the dusty road to the village that lay directly in their path, the latter seemed to glow with a surreal, though not unnatural, orange hue.

But even if nature had failed to deliver, the Wellingtonbridge Fair would have allayed any lingering doubts. Anyone who was anyone in the farming business attended 'The Well Fair'. This could be a lucrative five days. Now it must be remarked that the seeds of Home Rule were being sown, that the King was terminally insane and that we were at war both with France *and* with The United States of America. Yet the decade was a comparatively prosperous one for all that.

Approaching Wellingtonbridge from its western side, the trio continued on a straight course until reaching the structure from which the village derived its name. As they drew nearer and nearer to the said Wellington Bridge, they descried a solitary man leaning over its western wall. He was middle aged, of average height and rather lean. Shabbily dressed and with a weather-beaten visage, he stood chewing a piece of straw and squinting into the sunset. His complexion was ruddy and, facing westward, its ruddiness was all the more pronounced on account of his aspect just then.

"How yeh doin' good sir?" asked Michael Hendrick in as amicable a tone as he knew. "Anythin' doin' here, anythin' perhaps in the way of turnip-snaggin' for example?" he added, thereby revealing his trade to the stranger.

This stranger had noted with mild interest that Michael Hendrick carried by his side a small tool-bag. Its contents appeared, at least externally, as scarcely more than two or three small and jagged-edged farming implements, the extremities of which protruded slightly through the shabby brown cloth of which the tool-bag was woven.

"Turnip-snaggin'?" repeated the ruddy man shaking his head. "It's more in the bread-makin' line that I am, bein' at the fair for the corn deals if yeh take my meanin'."

With his gaze turned chiefly to the Corock River below, meandering as it did on its course to Bannow Bay and thence to the sea, the stranger had hitherto only tilted his head towards the visitors. But now he turned full towards them, straightened his posture and smiled as he extended a large, wrinkled, welcoming hand.

"Whitty's the name," he exclaimed adopting a more familiar tone. "Shay Whitty. It's barely a mile to th'east of the village that I live. And it's there I've dwelt, man and boy, some two score years and ten. Never missed the fair in all them years, me."

"Hendrick," returned the chief of the travellers, "Michael Hendrick," with a mild pretence at being pleased to make the man's acquaintance.

Whitty nodded towards the woman and the child.

"Ah, this is the wife Susanna, and our young child Megan-Leanne," added Hendrick without so much as a glance at either.

"Quare folk we've had callin' to the fair these last few autumns," continued Whitty reverting to his original pose on the western wall of the bridge. "Strange folk with stranger accents as yeh might say. We don't take kindly to quare folk in Wellingtonbridge, yeh know. But I'd say yer honest Wexford folk by yer talk. Into the village with yeh, and try yer luck. For it's worse yeh could be at nor snaggin' turnips. For as long as there's a harvest there'll be turnips, and as long as turnips, snaggin'."

Having thanked the stranger, the turnip-snagger and his family proceeded on their way and, turning to the left, directly entered the field around which all the excitement and activity of the event seemed to centre. For the most part the green itself was girdled by a long, continuous, ridge of grass. This knoll—some three feet high—constituted a sort of boundary with the river, the latter flowing in such a manner as to half-encircle the field in a sort of horse-shoe shape before passing under the bridge.

It being early evening, the serious dealings of the day had all been concluded some time ago. Yet the fair was none the more subdued for it. For as the livestock and equipment trading of the day had drawn to a close, and as the various traders tidied their respective stalls with an air of finality—Friday being the last full day of the fair—the evening's entertainment commenced. As neither of our pedestrians had much heart for an encounter with palm-readers, fortune tellers or such like, they scanned the field for a suitable refreshment tent among the many there present. Two, which stood nearest to them in the haze of the failing sunlight, seemed almost equally inviting. One was flagged "Stout, Ale and good Local Brew." On the other appeared the placard "Wholesome Soup Here." Having weighed both inscriptions in his mind, Michael Hendrick's leaning was to the former.

"Soup is good 'n' nourishing after a long hard day's walking Michael," protested the woman in a soft yet determined voice. "Besides, little Megan takes well to it."

Having grunted his disapproval, her husband acquiesced to her representations notwithstanding and they entered all three into the soup tent.

Two long and narrow tables lined the walls of this rectangular tent. At one end stood a stove containing a charcoal fire over which hung a large three-legged crock. The scene was presided over by a toothless crone. This hag, who must have seen about sixty winters, cackled inanely as she slowly stirred the contents of the pot. Having entered the tent and proceeded towards this end, Michael Hendrick slowed his pace considerably as he overheard a fellow traveller enquiring as to the contents of the soup. Straining his ears to overhear the reply, he surmised that the slop that was for sale here was comprised largely of such ingredients as carrots, potato and onion, among others.

Three bowls, two large and one small, of this steaming hot mixture were ordered and the family sat down to consume them and take their ease for a time. The uninviting appearance of the stuff or the unsavoury odours lingering on the surface of each bowl might have deterred one unaccustomed to such rustic culinary tastes. Yet, as one who is full loathes honey so to the hungry even what is bitter tastes sweet.

But there was more in that tent than met the eye. Michael Hendrick had suspected, from the very moment he set eyes on the soup woman, that such virtues as honesty and integrity may have been wanting in her. They certainly were. For when he'd devoured his first bowl full he winked to her as he returned his basin. Thereupon, the old hag discreetly produced a large bottle from under the table, clandestinely measured out a quantity of its contents and tipped it into the man's soup. The liquor poured in was whiskey. The secret manner in which she performed this act was equalled only by the secrecy with which the grateful customer promptly paid for the favour. This strongly spiked cocktail was vastly more to his satisfaction than had been the original mixture in its natural state. His wife had observed the proceedings with a degree of uneasiness. Yet after a time he had quashed her protestations and even convinced her to sample some herself. Susanna agreed, but only to half a bowl—and of a far milder dose at that.

As her husband ordered further helpings of this heavily laced concoction, and as it told more on his manner and his conduct just then, Susanna Hendrick mused on the choices before them some two hours before. Having successfully kept her family out of the licensed liquor-tent next door she deemed that they were at present in a potentially more perilous environment among these irregulars and smugglers. Yet an even greater consideration was on her mind and had been for some hours—that of a lodging for the night. Not once did she remind her husband that it might be a struggle to find suitable lodgings in Wellingtonbridge on this the last night of the fair. Yet as the hours were wasted thus she knew it would soon be well nigh impossible.

The child stirred impatiently. It is one of those subtle essences of human nature that weariness, which typically quietens an adult and causes him to withhold all unnecessary utterances, will invariably have precisely the opposite effect on those of more tender years. As the hours passed and dusk yielded to darkness, agitation sat visibly on the face of Megan-Leanne. Her mother raised the challenge once again, this time in a louder voice, "Michael, what about our lodging? You know we may have trouble in getting it if we don't try soon."

The husband, thereupon, dismissed her protestations as tedious. The more of the laced soup he ingested the more expostulatory the man became. He had consumed just that quantity of alcohol that so often causes a man to project his views into his companions' hearing in as argumentative a tone of voice as possible, irrespective of whether his companions are in agreement with him or not. The conversation in which he was so engrossed evolved onto the subject of marriage. The half-dozen or so men directly involved in this intriguing discourse seemed to concur on one issue; the tragic nullification of a young man's ambitions, the wasteful usurping of his energies, and the unending regrets that haunt him as a direct consequence of an early and overhasty marriage.

"Worst mistake I ever made or ever will," Michael Hendrick insisted, thumping his large hand on the bench in a resentful and self-accusatory manner. "Married at nineteen, me, ah." He buried his head in his hands and gently but firmly thumped his forehead on the bench. His words were at such a volume that it would have been impossible for his young wife to miss any of them.

Nor was that his intention. Indeed, Susanna acted as one well nigh accustomed to such derogation from her spouse. One of the six companions, a hay-trusser from Foulkesmill called Kinsella, enquired of Hendrick the reason for his haste in committing lifelong to a woman he'd only known some months, and for whom he had an affection that seemed at best scanty. Hendrick pointed at the young child, now fast asleep despite the clamour, and the farmer nodded slowly.

Michael Hendrick continued, "I'm a man of eighteen shillings and no more. Yet no mean hand in my trade. I'd challenge Leinster, let alone Wexford, to beat me in the turnip-snaggin' business. If I were unyoked once more I'd be worth every farthin' o' fifty pound by Christmas." He glanced sidelong at his wife and child and shook his head disingenuously, as if he were contriving the means of relinquishing his marriage vows, deeming them the cause of such great ruination in his life.

The conversation enjoyed a rare pause during which the guests on that side of the marquee could overhear, through its thin canvass, the conclusion of the fair's final transaction of the day. It was being negotiated very close by and sounded like the sale of an old horse at a knockdown price. It could readily be surmised from his cadences that the seller was a member of the itinerant community—a people renowned for conducting no small measure of trade in the line of horses.

Hendrick reflected on this transaction and, in his drunken state, announced "I can't see why a good honest man shouldn't get rid of a wife he don't want as these tinker folk do their auld horses, why shouldn't they put them up for auction eh? Why not? To men who desire as much? Hey? Why?"

"And you'd be putting yer own up?" asked the hay-trusser jovially, lifting his own soup bowl to his lips.

"I surely would!" exclaimed Michael Hendrick unexpectedly standing up, "if anyone's desperate enough t'ave her. And who'll start the biddin'? Eh? Here's a chance yeh can't pass-up." He glanced around the tent. As he did so an eerie silence fell. Only the turnip-snagger's own unsympathetic and half slurred voice could be heard.

"Michael," said his wife sternly, "you're at it again, there's times I almost think you mean it."

"I surely do, woman," he sneeringly replied.

The silence grew. His wife was well used to this kind of careless banter from her heartless husband but she had a foreboding that he was taking it too far on this occasion. Hitherto, the challenge had always died a natural death as those present perceived no real intention to follow through on this most preposterous and shameful of transactions. Susanna protested again and again, more grimly each time. The more she protested, the more determined her defiant husband seemed to be to drive this dangerous auction towards its conclusion, with incalculable results for all concerned.

"Any buyers?" shouted Michael Hendrick again glancing around the tent with, feigned or real, a marked expression of anticipation written across his face. "Will anybody buy her?"

"I wish someone would now, Mike!" said she firmly. "At least I'd be free of you, my excuse for a husband."

"And I free of you, my burden of a wife," he returned. The uncanny atmosphere that permeated the tent was palpable just then—a strange combination of wonder and incredulity throughout. This kind of trade was heard of in those days, but such transactions were few and far between. Was a wife to be sold in Wellingtonbridge? And sold at the fair and all? Soon an auctioneer was appointed and lingering doubts about this callous young man's intentions were laid to rest.

"Any ailments upon her?" shouted one man with a distinctly foreign accent. "Ye can't be selling a bad horse to a Scotsman?"

"Not a spec," replied Michael Hendrick, "she's fit as a fiddle yeh might say."

"How many years on her?" cried another.

"She's the wan age o' me," came the succinct reply.

"Yeh don't make mention o' the child," cried a local youth, barely old enough himself to marry and seemingly posing the question out of mere curiosity. "Is she in the bargain too?"

"Every bit of her," replied the husband, seemingly prepared for the question.

"Who'll bid three pound?" asked the auctioneer in a booming voice. Michael Hendrick swiftly glanced at the man with a look of grave admonition. Were his goods to be valued at a mere three pounds? No words were necessary. The turnip-snagger's look was sufficient. The auctioneer promptly added another pound.

"Nottin' less than five!" cried the turnip-snagger in his usual, uncompromising, fashion. "For I'll be damned if that's not a bargain. Five pound and she's yours. Five pound and tonight's the last yel see o' me. Five pound, any takers?"

"Five pound, come along now," shouted the auctioneer as if his services would soon be deemed superfluous to the transaction. "Yeh heard the young man. Five pound for his wife, the child 'n' all, last chance, or she'll be withdrawn."

"*Four* and *ten*," exclaimed a tall man from the far end of the table. The silence was deafening. The man stood up. He was burly and his attire revealed that he was a sailor by trade. All eyes fell on this intriguing stranger who had hitherto remained silent and now that business seemed to be for real and not for show had actually announced his bid.

"Four and ten yeh say?" questioned the husband, eying the sailor.

"Not a farthin' less, not a farthin' more," came the sailor's reply.

"Time to show yeh mean it. Out with the money."

The sailor moved closer to the woman and her child. Having inspected both and satisfied himself as to the value of the deal, he unfolded four crisp pieces of paper and singularly counted them out onto the surface of the wooden table. They were genuine Bank of Ireland £1 banknotes. To these were added four half-crowns. To most there present, the sight of such sums was wholly new. In sheer disbelief did the spectators observe what was unfolding before them. Keen eyes were turned now to the seller, now to the buyer, now to the wife with her young child, now to the money resting on the table. Any remaining suspicion that this had all been a mere frivolous jape was instantly dispelled by the appearance of the several notes and coins. Those that had laughed off the evening's proceedings as the mere eccentricity of a disheartened, unemployed, frustrated and drunk young turnip-snagger, now fell silent as the next move was eagerly anticipated by all.

"Mike!" cried the wife, with a sombre expression, "so much as smell those banknotes and I go with the sailor, me and Megan-Leanne too. Your joke is over."

"Joke? Oh it's no joke I'm at woman. I takes the cash. The sailor takes you. Sure nottin' could be simpler."

The deal was concluded inside mere seconds. The sailor's money was taken and safely stowed. The sailor addressed Susanna in a kindly tone and soon the new couple were at the door of the tent. Susanna did pause briefly upon exiting, but only to remove her wedding ring and hurl it the entire length of the tent directly in her husband's face. The man was mildly startled as the small but symbolic piece of jewellery struck him at his breast pocket, rolled down his arm, bounced off the wooden table and into what remained of his last helping of soup.

Somehow there was a cruel irony in where fate had directed the ring that was not lost on all those present. But the observers were awestricken to a man, having never witnessed anything like it. The more whiskey-laden soup the man had temerariously consumed the more that same concoction had threatened to consume his marriage. It was an end to the evening that even he had not foreseen and, in his drunken stupor, had not yet fully dawned on him in all its finality. After some minutes Michael Hendrick advanced to the door of the tent as if to satisfy himself as to the departure of the newly constituted family.

"Sure it's well cared for she'll be," cried a woman in the tent, "bein' in the hands of a nice sailor as him. Looks like he have a few bob too, more than the poor soul's been used to I'll warrant."

"Well, she's gone," said Michael Hendrick as he sat down again with an air of resignation, "and I'll not be chasin' her. Watch me. Do yeh see me chasin' her? Not me. But she took the girl as she's no business doin'. It's me that's the father o' that maid, not some sailor. She'd no right to take her, I tell yeh."

It now being late and the sun having well set folk began vacating the tent. Even the soup woman started to gather up her things and, by degrees, bring that day's commerce to an end. By this time Hendrick was seated on the floor with his back against the wall in a dark corner of the tent. He reclined a little as if dozing.

Minutes later the soup woman observed his state and perceiving him to be by now fast asleep left him undisturbed. For as the fair was to continue into Saturday—albeit a half-day and only attended by a smattering of locals in search of a few late bargains—the marquee was to remain undisturbed for another twelve hours until such time as a general clean-up began the following afternoon. Soon Hendrick and the old hag were the only two souls remaining. The latter then extinguished the last candle, exited the tent and drove away into the moonless night.

CHAPTER 2

❦

First Regrets

Scarcely a noise could be heard when Michael Hendrick awoke. Outside, there was the remote and indistinct sound of birds whistling in trees, the occasional bleating of far off sheep or the distant bark of a dog somewhere in the village. Hendrick opened his eyes and glanced around him. He stared for a time at a brown bundle under one of the long tables, then recognised it as his own bag of tools. He noticed the stove where the soup had been mixed, the empty bowls out of which it had been consumed and various other oddments strewn around the floor.

Suddenly he could discern a small shiny object amongst all the bits and bobs—his wife's ring. Slowly he began to recount in his mind, as best he could, the events of the preceding night. He recalled the long table and could identify the exact stool where he'd sat. He was reminded of the taste of the laced soup. Though he was just then suffering from its dyspeptic side effects he couldn't begin to reckon how much he had consumed. Then small portions of dialogue began to stream into his mind. He remembered the course that the conversation had taken, and then seemed to recollect something about his wife being for sale in some auction or other. Was it a dream, a mere whimsical fancy of his, or was it reality? Which, he could not tell.

After several seconds more of debating which events were real and which imagined, his right hand suddenly clasped his breast pocket. At that very moment the enormity of what he had done dawned fully on his consciousness. There in his breast pocket were the four crisp £1 notes that the sailor had paid him. The four half-crowns also jangled in his pocket when he struck it. He closed his eyes, took a deep breath, and clasped his pocket even tighter. Each minute that passed, as well as each particle of evidence found, seemed to sober him up a little more. Sober enough to walk at any rate, he collected his tool-bag, flung it over his shoulder and noiselessly opened the tent door.

Were it not for the burdensome predicament into which Michael Hendrick had negligently propelled himself the night before he might have been better placed to enjoy the freshness of a September sunrise in Wellingtonbridge. It was still an early hour, not long after seven, and the autumn morning's rich stillness was broken only by the occasional shuffle of the slumbering tinker folk who had snugly wrapped themselves in heavy bed cloths for a night's sleep in their carts.

Silently, Hendrick advanced to the fair-field's exit. Upon reaching the gate, he glanced in both directions. To his right and the west, lay the bridge he had traversed at dusk—this time with no Shay Whitty. To his left and the east lay the village centre in all the meditative inertness of an autumn daybreak. The dawn haze had shrouded Wellingtonbridge in a sort of picturesque nebulosity that the waxing sun soon dispelled.

He determined to leave Wellingtonbridge unseen by a single observer. In consideration of which he opted to travel in a southerly direction. He strode away southbound towards the quiet town-land of Maudlintown, heeded only by a large ginger cat that stared at him from the corner of a barn roof. He had perched himself there for the sole purpose of taking pleasure in the rays of the morning sun. The turnip-snagger passed Maudlintown and continued walking for about a country mile. In his capricious compunction, he contemplated and reflected on his reckless act. Its rashness, its impetuousness and sheer irreversibility gnawed at him in all their starkness and filled him with self-loathing. What had he done? How long would it take to make reparations if indeed reparation could ever really be made for such deeds? These questions, and a hundred like them, Michael Hendrick churned over and over in his mind as he walked along. The mere thought of his rash deed smote him with remorse and despair.

Presently, he reached another bridge at which he resolved to take a short rest, the rather to decide on his next move than for any reasons of fatigue. He had arrived at Waterloo Bridge whereupon he turned sidelong into a narrow lane, unshouldered his bag, threw it on a still dewy patch of grass at the side of the lane and sat down with a sigh.

After some thought he convinced himself that he had not made known his surname to anyone at the fair. He was conscious that he'd introduced himself by name on one occasion but that was only to the stranger on the bridge, Shay Whitty. This did not concern him. Filled with self-pity, he resolved to place the blame for his misdemeanour on his erstwhile wife. *She* had been sober. *She* had had all her wits about her as joviality descended into folly, and when basin after basin of laced soup had been downed by her incautious husband. Why didn't she stop him? She knew only too well the nature of his conduct when he drank, having witnessed it many times before. She could have stopped it. She *should* have stopped it. It was an unguarded moment of madness that may not be atoned for in an entire lifetime.

Minutes later he gathered his wits and resolved to search for her. In the energy of his distress he would search high and low, attempting to ferret out both his wife and his young daughter Megan-Leanne. Nothing would deter him. He would reclaim his family whatever the risk to himself. The shame of what he had done he would just have to live with. But first he would undertake to swear an oath. Yes, this was his most immediate priority just then.

About a mile to the east of Waterloo Bridge lay the village of Carrick-on-Bannow, the very village where his wife had been born some twenty-one summers earlier. His resolve was strong and his purpose firm. He would go to the village and there, in whatever setting seemed appropriate to him, take his vow. The landscape surrounding Carrick was largely featureless. On his walk southwards from Wellingtonbridge he had observed the odd ancient castle along with farms and fields on his left, while to his right lay the still waters of Bannow Bay. But not until he reached Carrick did he catch sight of any setting that might serve as a fitting location for his oath-taking. Then, as if it had been drawing him to itself, he observed a cemetery. Still and peaceful on that calm sunny morning, it lay before him with its gate half open. Entering as silently as he could to avoid unnecessarily arousing suspicion he walked to a small cross-shaped pond at the centre of the graveyard and knelt. In a state of extreme contrition for his great error he said aloud the following words,

"I, Michael Hendrick, on this morning of Saturday the tenth of September in the year of Our Lord eighteen hundred and fourteen, do take a solemn oath to The Sacred Heart o' Jesus that I will purpose to avoid all alcoholic beverages for a period of twenty-one years."

Hendrick rose, made the sign of the cross, and exited the cemetery. The magnitude of the task facing him slowly became apparent. Leaving Carrick, he walked for another hour along the eastward road until he reached a small village called Duncormick. There, after a few morsels of food for breakfast—for it was nearly midday and he'd eaten and drunk nothing since the soup—the turnip-snagger proceeded in a south-easterly direction until he happened upon a small fishing village. He figured that, if his wife had been adopted by a sailor, he might hope to find her in so maritime a location.

The name of the fishing village was Kilmore Quay. It was a quant village where most of the activity centred on the harbour. Out to sea, scarcely more than a league off the coastline and clearly visible on such an afternoon, rose the picturesque Saltee Islands, uninhabited and untroubled—at least by human life. To the west lay a desolate lagoon in which many sea birds and other wildlife had endeavoured to make their habitat. To the east were some low cliffs and a long sandy beach stretching for some miles. Kilmore Quay was snugly nestled between the two and, though a small village, its importance to the county's fishing industry could not be overstated. Day after day, net loads of whiting, trout, codling, mackerel, plaice, pouting—and many more species besides—were hauled ashore at Kilmore Quay.

Hendrick was in the rather embarrassing quandary of having to relate to locals the appearance of the folk he so earnestly sought, yet without offering any details of how these peculiar circumstances had arisen. After about two hours of going hither and thither in the village, enquiring of this person and of that, Hendrick finally happened on his first clue. A protracted conversation with a local fishmonger eventually revealed to him that a mail boat containing several passengers, three of which precisely matched his descriptions, had left the harbour that very midday for the afternoon sailing to Queenstown. At the mention of Queenstown Hendrick's heart sank and he was visibly shocked. Every hour that passed seemed to drive home to him the gravity and irrevocability of what he done the previous evening. Queenstown was no small fishing harbour, no inconsequential little village somewhere down the coast. If anything, it was the opposite. For it was from the Port of Queenstown that many folk had set sail on a one-way journey, for good or ill, to far flung parts in North America.

Hendrick thanked the fishmonger and gloomily stared at the ground. Less than twenty-four hours earlier he had a wife and a young daughter by his side. Now the stark realisation dawned on him that within days—yes perhaps sometime that very month—those two would be a thousand leagues away. They would be a new family with new hopes, settling into a new life on a new continent. He buried his head in his hands as a feeling of utter despondency pervaded every part of his being.

Gathering his thoughts again, he ambled along the beach for a mile or two. What would he do now? Would his wife ever return? The thought even occurred to him that it might have been the sailor's very intention that Hendrick learned of their sailing to Queenstown and thus be thrown off their scent. Perhaps they would simply come ashore and settle somewhere in Ireland. However, he soon dismissed this notion as a mere fantasy. Time lagged wearily. As late afternoon turned to dusk he found lodgings in the nearby district of Bastardstown. It was the first really cool night of autumn and the common room of the farmhouse where Hendrick secured his lodging had a small fire in the hearth. He stared into the fire as he took his frugal supper—farmhouse bread with cheese and a mug of tea—then retired to his room where he climbed into bed and fell into an uneasy sleep.

The next morning, Michael Hendrick set out for the district in which he had resolved to settle. He broke his fast at eight o'clock and, journeying northeastward, did not pause until he reached Ferrycarrig. Many bridges spanned the River Slaney in those days but Ferrycarrig was the furthest point downstream at which one could cross without incurring a toll. Sharp, rugged, cliff-like features rose majestically on either side of the river. Nestled at the foot of the western cliff, as though it had been hewn out of the rock, stood a solitary public house. As Michael Hendrick felt the need of something to refresh him just then he found the meagre inn congenial enough to that end. Having taken his lunch the traveller then took some minutes to further rest from his journeying. The proudness of Ferrycarrig Castle as it glowered imperiously at passersby—coupled with the august, almost imperturbable serenity with which the River Slaney gently curved and rambled its way to its estuary—had a restorative effect on the traveller. His energies were at any rate rekindled in sufficient measure to drive him purposefully on to the final leg of his long-planned journey.

He traversed the bridge to proceed in a northward direction, skirting the vast estate known as Saunderscourt Demesne. He turned eastward at Crossabeg and arrived a little later at the outskirts of a small town named Castlebridge, a neighbourhood that was to be his abode for the next quarter of a century.

CHAPTER 3

❁

Eighteen Years Later

The clamour of raised voices, the neighing of horses, the bleating of sheep in their pens and the general tumult of busy trade left no visitors to Wellingtonbridge in any doubt that it was the occasion once more for that most renowned of annual fairs. It was mid afternoon on Monday, the first day of the fair, and the general din and commotion of the day were at their climax. Countless farmers as well as numerous traders in agricultural equipment eagerly sought to capitalise on every conceivable opportunity for a good deal. Thus the market was in full swing.

But standing without the fair-field gate, almost unheeded by those within, stood two slim and tall women. Each wore a black cotton bonnet, a long black dress with black shawl, black gloves, a large black muff and black shoes. The older was a woman in her late thirties. Her face was lean and sunken, and for now wore an expression of quiet resoluteness. The younger woman, though about half her companion's age, was similar in appearance—and in more than dress. Yet her skin was of a more sallow texture, and her large round green eyes peered at her surroundings with an aloof inquisitiveness so archetypal of youth in unfamiliar surroundings. Few could have doubted that these two mourners were mother and daughter. They entered the fair-field and glanced about them at the various stalls dotted around.

"What do we mean by stopping in here?" asked the maiden in a soft voice. "Don't we wish to get onward soon?"

"We'll not stay long my dear Megan-Leanne but we have some unfinished business in this place that may just set us on our true course," came the mother's reply. "For it was in this place, this very field that I first met with Redmond all those years ago."

"What, you met father here? You mentioned you met him at a fair, but I've never been to a real fair before, at least any that I can remember. And I'm certain I've never been to the likes of Wellingtonbridge. So this is where my folks first met, is it?"

"It surely is," replied the mother.

As the maiden spoke a tear welled in her eye and she produced from her pocket a small card, bordered with black. One side bore the shape of a cross, and the other the following inscription:

> "In loving memory of Nicolas Redmond, sailor, who was so tragically lost at sea, in the month of August 1832, aged forty-five years. Rest in peace."

"Not only, dear daughter, was this fair the occasion for my meeting Nicky but this is also where we are going to look for that relative we're seeking, Mr. Michael Hendrick."

"You know mother, you've never really explained to me what exactly this Hendrick gentleman is to us. Is he a cousin? Is he a second cousin? I've never really been told it."

"Well, Megan-Leanne, let's just say for now that he is a relation by marriage," answered the mother.

"Not a close relative then?"

"Nothing of the sort."

"Don't suppose he ever knew me?" continued the persistent daughter.

"Quite right," came the succinct reply.

"But mother," continued Megan-Leanne, "you told me it was many years ago, and surely different folks attend the fair over the years, coming and going as time and chance allow. Sure I'll wager that you're the one solitary soul at the fair today that was here all those years ago."

"I wouldn't be too confident about that," admonished the mother. "Look carefully towards the top of the field. Just there on the left near the ridge, what do you see?"

The daughter turned her gaze in that general direction. What could be seen in the location described was a large pot suspended from one of the lower branches of a tree. But as the two advanced they detected smoke emanating from the place. Beneath the pot was a small fire of wood. At the scene sat a miserable wretch of a woman dressed in rags and holding a large spoon. Decrepit, hoary and senescent in the extreme, the old hag sat alone dribbling as she muttered something to herself in a voice barely audible. Occasionally, a large wheezy breath was inhaled and the old gammer squawked in a voice too fiendish to be believed, "Wholesome soup here." It was indeed the old soup woman from all those years ago. Having fallen on harder times, she seemed to have lost both her tent and her tables, as well as much of her custom.

"Now, my daughter, *she* was here for a start. We'll go and talk to her," said the mother.

"We'll do no such thing," protested the daughter. "Good respectable folk as us seen talking to her?"

"O.K. my dear, *I'll* go and talk to her. You can wander about the stalls if you like."

This plan was far more agreeable to Megan-Leanne. At least she was to be spared the ordeal of being included one way or another in such an irksome interchange, with all the social embarrassment that that was to cause to a well-raised young maiden on the threshold of adulthood. Meanwhile her mother approached the soup woman and noticed, with some discomfiture, that she herself was being croaked at by the woeful beldam at some ten or fifteen yards off. Business had clearly suffered greatly in the intervening eighteen years and the soup woman dealt out a bowlful of the simmering slop for her client with the enthusiasm of one clearly desperate for every farthing of custom.

"Business been happier in bygone days, I'll warrant?" remarked the customer candidly.

"It surely was, ma'am," replied the soup woman directly. "Yeh say right, for it's half a century I'm in this line yeh know. And it's outside hearty helpin's o' soup the fair's folk have been puttin' themselves all that time, and at these hands too."

"Indeed," observed the customer, "and all from this little setting in the corner of a field?"

"Not a bit of it!" retorted the soup woman. Then leaning forward and lowering her voice, she explained, "yel not believe this, but upon a time I was the owner of an immense marquee, one as stretched some fifty yards, where year after year me benches were filled up with folk after a sample of the tasty and wholesome soup."

"Can you recollect," asked Susanna, "the selling of a wife by her husband, as happened in that very tent some eighteen years ago yesterday?"

The old wretch began to slowly shake her head. She stared at the ground and mused for about thirty seconds. Then suddenly glared at Susanna Redmond as if she were indeed reminded of some long ago deal that had raised a hue and cry at the time, but about which few remarks had been heard ever since. "Yeh know, ma'am. I can't help meself recallin' somethin' o' the sort. Would it have been to a mariner type lad, by chance?"

"The very same," came Susanna's answer, "to a sailor, mid twenties, by the name of Nicolas Redmond."

"Every bit of it!" replied the crone. "Funny, I'd scarcely o' remembered it only the husband came back the very next year. He told me if his wife ever return and enquire where he's gone to tell her he's gone to…eh…now what's the name of the place he said?"

"Think!" enjoined Susanna with a great deal more urgency in her voice than before. "Where was it? Think hard."

"Ere, let me think," replied the soup woman, "was it Campile?…no, t'wasn't there…ere, where did he say now? 'Twas seventeen year ago yeh know, and th'aul' memory is not what it used to be. Not Campile then nor Clonroche ayther. Was it the likes o' Curracloe? Or somewhere i' that neck o' the woods I seem to recall." The old hag tapped her fingers on her spoon for several more seconds before exclaiming in confident tones, "Castlebridge! *That's* where he said. 'Twas Castlebridge, sure as I'm standin' here."

Susanna Redmond may have had in mind to reward the pitiful dotard with some small token of her appreciation. But she was all too conscious of the fact that it was by that unprincipled woman's concoction her husband had been profligated. Instead she nodded thankfully and repaired to Megan, who'd been scanning some of the nearby stalls.

"Auld sinner she may be but from that woman I've learnt what I set out to," remarked Susanna to her daughter. "If our relative is still alive, and God willing let it be, then he's most likely living in the vicinity of Castlebridge. Now Castlebridge is a quare long distance from here Megan-Leanne, some six leagues or more, yet I think it's there we should make for."

It was obvious to both parties that, for such a distance, some class of conveyance would need to be arranged in advance. So they set about procuring two carriage seats for the morrow's journey northeastward then retired to their lodging.

That night, as she lay uneasily in bed staring blankly at the ceiling Susanna Redmond dwelt on all that had befallen the family during the past eighteen years. On the day immediately following the fateful night at the fair the three had indeed sailed to Queenstown in County Cork. Bustling port that it was Redmond had immediately happened upon gainful employment in that place and the family opted to remain there for a time. Susanna was unconditionally devoted to her new husband. But her devotion owed little to the sailor's geniality and kindly manner and more to her own simple nature. Uneducated, unenlightened and blindly obedient to the social convention of the day, Susanna believed the status of every wife was as a husband's property. Irregular though the transaction at the fair had been, Nicky Redmond had parted with a handsome sum of money for her and she felt bound to him for it.

The following year Redmond's work took them back to County Wexford and they settled in New Ross for about fourteen years. Redmond found himself increasingly involved in transatlantic trade and, in the spring of eighteen twenty-nine the family emigrated to Canada to the coastal, French-speaking town of Rivière-du-Loup.

Then after three years of relative prosperity news reached Susanna and her daughter that Nicky Redmond had been lost at sea. From what they could glean this accident had happened some fifty or so leagues off the southwest coast of Greenland, somewhere between the Labrador Sea and the Davis Straight. Notwithstanding all the economic uncertainly that might have plagued the two women as a consequence of their calamitous loss, Susanna Redmond began to bend her thoughts ever more deliberately on her original and legal husband. Here was a woman of surpassing naivety. Even now with the sailor dissevered from her, she was not emancipated. She convinced herself that she was still in Heaven's eyes the wife of one Michael Hendrick, and would remain so while he lived. For Susanna Redmond, marriage was 'until death do ye part'. Just as the contract sealed at Wellingtonbridge had only matured upon the loss of the sailor, so her own Marriage Contract was solemn and binding until death. She'd learnt of the sailor's drowning and within days had resolved to return to Ireland with her daughter. They'd settle wherever seemed fitting and would search for Hendrick by whatever means they deemed appropriate.

Susanna had, for a time, contemplated reverting to her maiden name of MacMurrough, but then reconsidered and deemed it imprudent. She was perceived as the legal widow of Nicky Redmond so a Redmond she would remain for now. Such considerations mattered little, however, when measured against that most pertinent of questions. Was all to be revealed to her daughter whom she cherished so affectionately? Megan-Leanne was a young adult now so the revelation should have a less destabilising effect on the girl than at an earlier more impressionable age. And yet, every year that passed by was another year that Megan grew in blissful ignorance of the truth.

After much internal deliberation Susanna Redmond decided rather to keep the truth from her daughter. So it was that the maiden would continue to believe, in adult life as she had in childhood, that the relations between her mother and the sailor were those of a regularly married couple.

CHAPTER 4

❦

Of Mills and Grown Barley

By mid-afternoon the following day mother and daughter had reached the outskirts of Castlebridge. Having dismounted their northbound carriage at Kyle Cross some three miles west of their destination, the two made the final stage of their journey on foot. The undulating nature of the surrounding country allowed those destined for Castlebridge to scan the roofs of its more lofty constructions at a distance of some half a league off. But from such a perspective those rooftops appeared as scarcely more than a disordered medley of greys. Little of the town's real business could be espied from its outskirts and this owed largely to the expanse of tall trees that seemed to environ it from every side. The only distinct views enjoyed by the travellers just then both lay to their right. There were rolling bog lands through which a number of small tributaries steadily swirled their way into the River Slaney's estuary. Beyond the water was Wexford Town, the commercial and administrative centre of the county.

As soon as they had reached the Poulsack Bridge, the fast-flowing River Sow purling beneath, both women turned sidelong into a laneway and took their ease for a time. Susanna was acutely aware of the possibilities that lay before her. She may enter the town to find little or no trace of her first husband. Perhaps he *had* lived at Castlebridge some seventeen years earlier but had tragically met his end shortly afterwards. Perhaps he'd had the misfortune to fall victim to some foul disease or to some misadventure involving the employment of newly invented farming machinery—a fate not uncommon in those days as too many rural records show. The thought even occurred to her that

Hendrick might actually have drunk himself into an early grave. Yet in spite of his reckless nature it seemed just as probable that he had made a relative success of rebuilding his life. Susanna had detected nothing in the soup woman's tone that would suggest her husband had degraded himself any further in the twelve months immediately following their separation. He was only twenty-two that year so perhaps, throughout the prime of life, his renowned turnip-snagging skills had stood him in good stead. His being remarried did however seem improbable, owing chiefly to the arduous civic representations required on his part to substantiate any claim to bachelorhood.

Shouldering their travelling baskets once more, the two women continued on their way and duly entered the town proper. They did so along the western road known as Codd's Walk. Earlier in the century several key engineering projects had been undertaken with the ambition of bearing Castlebridge's local infrastructure into the nineteenth century. Chief among these endeavours was the construction of the impressive 'Castlebridge Canal' some two decades earlier. The commercial life of Castlebridge had since been transformed as barges could now be navigated the half-mile or so from the estuary below directly into the town centre—a feat hitherto deemed impracticable by the shallow and meandering nature of the River Wire. No fewer than six of the engineers assigned to this enterprise were Codd brothers. Each evening after work those half-dozen tired but hardy men could be observed returning to their homes in the northwestern precinct of the town. Some few years later the western road was renamed 'Codd's Walk' in honour of that acclaimed family's contribution.

As the two women proceeded thus towards the town centre the residential nature of Codd's Walk was not lost on either. Solitary dwelling places had occasionally been observed on the last mile or so of their journey, but now both women knew full well that they had arrived in Castlebridge for real. Even as they walked that short highway, straight and level as it was, local residents peered snoopily at them from over garden fences and modest hedgerows. Yet within minutes Mrs. Redmond and her daughter had put the avenue behind them. Halting for a time they observed how the road suddenly veered to the right and downhill. Where Codd's Walk had ended the town's Main Street began and any newcomers were then afforded a commanding view of the town centre.

Never in her wildest imaginings had Mrs. Redmond pictured Castlebridge as a place of such prodigious commercial activity. A supply service of grocers, coal yards, pubs and eating-houses lined either side of the Main Street. Castlebridge even had its own hotel, 'The South Leinster Arms'.

Strolling down Main Street mother and daughter passed by these outlets, and more besides. Some yards to their left they could see the tastefully designed Castlebridge House, extended by its dome-shaped and opulently picturesque conservatory. Before long the street levelled off, taking them towards the southern end of the town. They soon arrived at a bridge over a narrow canal. Aware that the estuary lay on their right—some mile or two to the west—both women directed their glances upstream to their left in an attempt to establish precisely where the canal would lead. They scarcely needed to look far. About a hundred yards to their left was a large mill wheel behind which stood a colossal milling complex. Near the foot of this enormous complex stood several long barges at which merchants were busily loading and unloading all manner of farm produce. Wheat, oats, hay and especially barley seemed chiefly to be what was traded, and in no small measure.

In those days Castlebridge boasted around five malting houses while the mill employed several dozen of the local townsfolk. Shortly after the official opening of the renowned Castlebridge Canal a toll was levied on all merchant vessels sailing under Wexford Bridge. Several merchants defiantly refused to pay a single farthing of the highly controversial tax, whereupon Wexford Town Corporation duly filed a legal suit against them. But Irish courts readily dismissed the case and declared the toll illegal. The commercial life of Castlebridge was radically transformed as a direct consequence. By the eighteen-thirties it was rated as one of the biggest and most important villages in Ireland, let alone Wexford, and was recognised as a thriving commercial centre of a class seldom met. Shelmaliere East may have been the smallest of the county's nine baronies, yet where economic success was concerned it suffered no rival. A hugely prosperous community had grown out of what had become an inland port in its own right.

Susanna Redmond and her daughter turned once again toward the Main Street. The folding of trading-stalls, the raising of shutters, the locking up of shop-fronts and a general clamour on the street told that the hour had arrived for the day's business in Castlebridge to draw to its close. It was by now early evening and the two women had each an appetite on them. Among the townsfolk going to and fro at that busy time was a group of three young men, not much older than Megan-Leanne. All three were scantily dressed and sat cross-legged on the ground passing an old tankard from one to the other. Mrs. Redmond and her daughter drew closer to the trio until both began to descry more accurately what was afoot.

Sitting thus the three were sampling ale and audibly deliberating on everything from its appearance to its aftertaste. Approaching the scene Mrs. Redmond enquired of this company the location of a reputable inn, yet one suited to those of modest means. The three young men then raised their glances to the visitors. Surveying the travellers for some moments and misreading their intentions, one of the party spoke.

"It's well ye'l be doin' to put yerselves outside some daycent beer in Castlebridge these days. We young labourers are hard put to it since all this barley trouble began, *very* hard put to it, not bein' able to get our hands on a hearty pint for love nor money."

Mrs. Redmond considered in her mind all what the phrase 'this barley trouble' might potentially amount to. Pleading ignorance in the matter, she quizzed the locals further. One replied forthwith.

"That scoundrel of a merchant's to blame if y'ask me. It's himself that all our millers and brewers buy off, and it's him that's after sellin' them growed barley. Ever seen what growed barley does to a pint o' beer? Why it's sour as can be. Born and bred in Castlebridge me, yet I never tasted the like of it before. But y'are strangers here for sure if it's askin' about the beer y'are at?"

"That we are," replied Mrs. Redmond. "Only arrived this last hour or so, and not a little hungry."

The two women soon withdrew to the opposite side of the street. When they were out of earshot, the three drinkers commented on the appearance of their chief visitor.

"'Not a little hungry' she says, and I'd well believe it," remarked one. "I've seen more mait on a butcher's knife."

"Never mind yer butchers knife," interjected another. "I've seen more on a Good Frida'!"

Aware that the evening was drawing in the travellers happened upon a fruit merchant on the point of closing his stall. Having procured some elementary refreshment there, at least enough to stave their appetites, they set about finding a lodging for the night. Having done so at an inn some hundred yards or so south of the canal bridge, Susanna Redmond suggested to her daughter that they venture into the town once more, this time unhindered by their travelling baskets, and search in earnest for their relative Mr. Michael Hendrick. Megan concurred.

Inside minutes the two women were out of their lodging house and striding back in the direction of the town centre. In the large open space that stood in front of the milling complex a significant crowd had gathered, and there was a general tumult that could be heard at some distance off. Hearing the raised voices and the general commotion Mrs. Redmond was disinclined to draw any closer, so the two women sat on a nearby bench for a time. Susanna proposed to her daughter that this public gathering, whatever its purpose, might suitably occasion the commencement of their search. Both women had a natural curiosity regarding this intriguing assembly, but Susanna appeared outwardly to be approaching the whole business with no small degree of dread. She spoke to her daughter gently.

"A large crowd seems to have gathered, don't you think? What a throng. I'll warrant there's prominent townsfolk in the centre of it, and the common folk of the neighbourhood gather 'round to hear. Don't you think Megan dear? Perhaps it's a convention of all the farming folk nearby and maybe they've shown up about all that barley trouble or whatever it is. Look, I'll sit here for a while and appear busy. Why don't you try to mingle and see if you can't garner any news of our relative. Try to discern in what esteem he's held in the town, you know, whether he's counted among the respectable folk or no. Don't be over-familiar now."

Megan-Leanne complied and walked towards the horde with a deliberate air of idle curiosity. She manoeuvred herself into the outer ring and stood for some minutes by the side of a large curly-haired man who was firmly grasping a hoe in his left hand. After some time at his side she ventured to talk to him.

"What's happening tonight?" enquired the girl.

"Stranger to Castlebridge then?" replied the local. "Haven't yeh heard anythin' of the dispute that's had the townsfolk in such a fash this last while?"

"Oh," replied Megan, "you mean all this business with the grown barley?"

"Of course, what else?" retorted the man, "nottin' of the sort's ever been put upon th'honest folk o' Castlebridge."

The maiden, with a little shuffling, finally managed to catch a glimpse of the folk at the very centre of this conference. On either side of a wooden table half a dozen or so large men appeared to be seated. What precisely they were engaged in at that moment Megan-Leanne could not readily ascertain. But at the top of the table, as though he were presiding over the others, stood an even larger man. He was some four or five inches above six feet. This man had a commanding presence and as commanding a voice. Around his neck hung a heavy golden chain that gave him the appearance of one currently in public office. It was at this man, who clearly enjoyed some position of authority or influence, that the majority of the townsfolk's questions appeared to be directed. He would raise his hand and answer a concerned local with a full and booming voice.

"I admit the bad barley," he said. "But I was deceived in buyin', no less than you brewers were who bought it off me."

"Meantime the poor townsfolk have ne'er a drop of daycent beer to comfort themselves wit'," protested a local.

"I'm even bein' blemt for the weather. Would yeh credit that? The whole county, let alone Castlebridge, knows how hard the weather was on us last harvest. At any rate seein' as how the business is gettin' too big to be run by meself alone, I'm after advertisin' for a manager, someone as knows his trade and can manage the barley end o' the business for me. Once he's in and settled, yel find no such mistakes bein' made again. Y'ave my word on it."

"What about the grown barley we've already got? Can we exchange it for a bit o' proper grain?" asked one local brewer.

"You show me, Mr. Wadding, how to turn grown barleycorn back into wholesome grain and I'll gladly oblige," came the sarcastic reply.

At this the assembly offered a collective groan of disapproval. Megan-Leanne stood for a time pondering on what she ought to do. The local miller's being addressed publicly as 'Mr. Wadding' was only the second time that evening she had learnt the family name of anyone in Castlebridge. The first was an hour earlier when the genial owners of 'The Pikeman's Inn', where she and her mother were to lodge that night, had cordially introduced themselves as Mr. and Mrs. Stafford. How she was to discreetly discover anything about a Hendrick, if indeed such a man still lived in that place, remained an enigma. Just then the man with the hoe spoke to her again, this time in more conciliatory tones.

"Can't help feelin' for the man, yeh know. Nice chap. Respected about the town too. First mistake he made in over three years as Mayor. Daycent aul' skin alright, never touches a drop yeh know, nottin' stronger than a cup o' tay. It's said that he made a vow upon a time, many year ago, that he'd not be tempted by a bottle o' stout for so many years. He never mentions it himself though. It's just a story put about the town over time. Yeh know what townsfolk are like."

Then another local man, overhearing this conversation, joined in by asking, "How many more years he got left of it Simon Lowney?"

"Two or three years at a guess. It's surely up soon anyway. Fair play for holdin' out so long is all I can say."

"True, true, yet it must keep him goin' all the same. I mean knowin' there's an end to't. Don't yeh think?"

"It surely does, Christy Colfer. I'll wager a lonely widow man as him looks forward to the day. Must be hard on a Frida' to watch his men all pourin' into the local taverns and he returnin' t'an empty house," replied Lowney.

"Men?" enquired Megan-Leanne, "Does he have many men working for him?"

"Many men? Why, fair maid, that man's the most influential member on the Corporation and with a good name in the county 'round besides. If it's wheat, barley, oats, hay, roots, and such like y'are dealin' in, he's yer man and no mistake. Sure he was nottin' when he came here them eighteen year back. Now he's a bastion o' the town, if yel not count this recent sorry business with bad barley that is. I seen the sun rise over Curracloe these nine-and-fifty year, yet ne'er before have I tasted ale as flat as has been made from Hendrick's barley. It's all growed out for sure. Bad barley."

"*Hendrick!*" exclaimed the girl, involuntarily raising her voice.

Simon Lowney and Christy Colfer stared at her inquisitively, both men mildly startled. The young woman soon gathered her wits and composed herself. "We were talkin' about the Mayor all along yeh know," explained Colfer, "or were yeh a little distracted just then?"

"No," replied Megan, "it's just that…no…it's OK…it's the Mayor, of course. Well I'd best be off gentlemen. Good night now." She hastily returned to her mother, the latter now standing and eagerly awaiting her daughter's tidings.

Lowney and Colfer stared at each other for some moments. Castlebridge enjoyed a reputation for the prettiest young girls in the county but even here this new face would turn many a head.

"Well Colfer, what do yeh make o' *her*?" enquired Lowney. "A fair young maid and no mistake."

"O indeed," replied his companion. "A munya maiden to be sure!"

Meanwhile Megan-Leanne had just returned to her mother at the bench.

"Glad news mother, oh very glad news. You'll hardly believe it it's that good," said Megan to her mother, barely able to contain her excitement.

"What my dear? Is our relation alive?…I mean, is he here?…I mean, oh, what's the news good daughter? Have you seen Mr. Hendrick?"

"Not only is he alive mother," replied the maiden catching her breath, "and not only is he living in Castlebridge, but you'll scarcely believe his good fortune. He seems from all accounts to be the head of a local business of great import. His line is in barley and oats and such like. I even heard he's got many men under him too. But that's not all. The most exciting thing of all is that Mr. Hendrick, that's our relative Mr. Michael Hendrick, is the Town Mayor!"

Megan-Leanne couldn't remember ever seeing anyone so visibly astounded in her life. Her mother sat down once more on the bench, doing so with a sigh that might have signified surprise, disappointment, incredulity or even mild amusement. How could a reckless man, a man so shameless and irresponsible as to sell his wife in a drunken stupor, ever rise to the position of Mayor? And how was it possible in so prestigious a town as Castlebridge? Surely the first ever Roman Catholic elected to the post. He was even directing an apparently successful grain business. For Susanna Redmond this almost defied belief and the whole affair was going to take some getting used to.

Megan, of course, could not for a moment have imagined how utterly incredible these tidings all seemed to her mother. Over the years she had learnt little of this man yet she had always been lead to believe somehow that this Mr. Hendrick, whoever he was, was unlikely to ever enjoy any kind of high standing in his local community. Susanna stared at the ground and whispered to herself the phrase 'Town Mayor' over and over and over again.

"I know mother, what a turn up, eh?" remarked Megan jovially. "That it should come to this. You even thought he might be dead. What a notion? And to find he's Mayor and all. Why it's queer as news from Bree."

Mrs. Redmond thanked her daughter for what she had gleaned. Just then the evening was getting on so both women decided to retire to their room at The Pikeman's Inn. The two joined hands and, with gentle affection, Megan-Leanne raised her mother to her feet. With that they repaired the short distance to their lodging.

CHAPTER 5

❀

Supper at The Pikeman's Inn

The walk from the town centre to The Pikeman's Inn was a short one. As has already been remarked this popular tavern was located on the southern side of Castlebridge, near to where the Blackwater Road met with the Ardcavan Road. Having thus passed on their right hand side the shop-fronts of Willy Prendergast the glazier, Donohoe the blacksmith, Sinnott the shoemaker, Keating the nail-maker and Morgan the saddler, the two travellers entered The Pikeman's Inn. Having been once more greeted upon their entrance by Mrs. Stafford they ascended to their room.

The Pikeman's Inn had a rather inviting appearance. The front of the building was almost entirely covered with ivy, a great deal of which would overhang the pretty Georgian windows of its rooms. The Pikeman's Inn was indeed reputed locally to be an establishment of moderate charges, but satisfactory too—displaying neither opulence nor paucity to any degree. Yet, given that the interior of the inn was both agreeable and rather commodious, Susanna Redmond began to wonder what the arguably subjective phrase 'moderate charges' amounted to in so prosperous a location as Castlebridge. She was at any rate concerned that she and her daughter might struggle to meet the tariff. The two women having discussed this for some minutes, Megan-Leanne ventured to make a proposal.

"Supposing I was to speak to Mr. and Mrs. Stafford directly. It sounds busy enough downstairs. Mr. Stafford's brew seems to be going down a treat."

Though The Pikeman's Inn was perennially popular, eighteen thirty-two was an especially lucrative year for that establishment. The recent surge in its popularity was easily accounted for. Its genial owner was a man of great foresight and, as a contingency against one bad harvest, had retained liberal quantities of barley from the scorching autumn of two years previous. The heavy downpours of the following September vindicated his strategy and, for the last twelve months, it was no secret that Mr. Stafford's was well nigh the only tavern in the barony selling a wholesome pint.

"Maybe there's an extra pair of hands needed and I could help out a little," continued the girl frankly. "Only the stoniest-hearted landlord wouldn't waive part of our accommodation for such favours, eh mother?"

"Oh Megan my gem of a daughter. Where would we be without you?" replied her mother with a gentle kiss of the young girl's forehead and in a tone that signified both gratitude and deep affection.

Megan-Leanne descended the stairs and eagerly sought the landlord. Unbeknownst to the young lady Stafford was in fact behind her on that same staircase, having just directed a newly arrived guest to his room. He smiled, duly wiped his hands on his large blue apron and spoke to the girl in affable tones.

"Ah, Miss Redmond. Settling in OK? Room to yer likin' and yer mother's too I trust?"

"Yes Mr. Stafford. We're very snug thank you. But I was just wondering, sir, if you could do with a little help this evening as you seem busy. I just though that it might go a little way toward our accommodation."

"Oh I see," replied Stafford. "Well yeh could say we're busy alright. But I could scarcely be sendin' as tender a maiden as yerself into the bar tonight. Oh miss, yed not credit some of the folks we get at The Inn in these days, boisterous as yeh might say. Still, such folks as pay for their stout and that's fine by me."

Megan-Leanne looked imploringly at the landlord. Mr. Stafford stared at the ceiling for a few seconds, thoughtfully scratched the underside of his chin and then nodded towards the girl.

"Tell yeh what," he said, "I'll not send y'into the bar at all but there's a guest in room four has just arrived from Kingstown. He's only here twenty minutes and I'll warrant he'd have an appetite on him somethin' fierce. Why it must be twenty-five leagues to Kingstown if it's a mile. Yeh could take him his supper. Mrs. Stafford will show yeh where everything is stored. Then later yeh could do the same for yerself and yer good mother, eh?"

This suggestion was well received by the young maiden and seemed propitious enough to the landlord's wife. Having procured the necessary victuals and arranged same on a supper tray in as presentable a manner as she knew how, the young girl climbed the stairs once more and gently knocked on the door of room number four.

"Come in," was the reply from inside the room. "Come on in."

At a table in front of the dresser sat a tall, fair haired, man of about thirty. His hair was straight and it occurred to Megan that it was also quite short for the period. The extensive locks on his cheeks were of a texture that was wavier (and of a hue that was rather more titian) than the hair on his head. Only when he stood to greet her did the young maiden realise how towering this young man was. Now Megan-Leanne Redmond was by no means a woman of small stature, being herself closer to six foot than to five. Yet this traveller seemed to have several inches on her, and wore an amicable expression as he gazed upon her attractive and graceful visage. But what of that? Megan had a face on which many eyes had turned and she was well used to this kind of admiration from the opposite sex. What were wholly new to her was this young man's accent and his mildly eccentric manner of speaking.

She had of course heard of the Port of Kingstown many times before, but only in the anecdotal form of sailors' stories told her by the recently departed man she had hitherto believed to be her father. This was the first time that she had actually met anyone from that place. She wondered if she would ever visit Kingstown in her life, how many of the country's seven million inhabitants lived in that town, how cosmopolitan a place it might be, how its locals might receive a simple country girl, and whether they all spoke like this man. The bizarre inflections and strange accentuations in his speech were altogether unfamiliar to the young girl. As he engaged her in conversation on the only two topics of any interest to him just then—his own supper and the next day's weather—she wondered to herself while such words as 'cheese-board' and 'ground-frost' were articulated with a deliberateness (and in a volume) scarcely deserved by such trivial matters. Never in her nigh-on score of years, three of which were spent on another continent, had she heard anything like it.

The guest confirmed that he had indeed travelled all the way from Kingstown that very day, and then duly introduced himself as one Robert Ferguson. The room allocated to him was situated at the front of the house. The young man stood for a time gazing out of the window and taking stock of his new surroundings. Observing the street below and the churchyard opposite, he explained that a new employment opportunity had brought him to Castlebridge and all that remained for him now was to secure his own place of accommodation. He was to start work first thing on the morrow as manager of Mr. Hendrick's barleycorn department. The Pikeman's Inn would suffice until he found his feet. This revelation greatly interested Megan-Leanne who, while carefully spreading his supper tray on the dresser, ventured to ask a favour of him.

"Mr. Ferguson sir, you mentioned that you are to be engaged at the mill from tomorrow and that you will be working for Mr. Hendrick as his kind of 'right-hand man' so to speak?"

"Yes, my dear, that's pretty much the extent of it."

"You're no doubt aware that presiding over a local business is not the only position of authority that Mr. Hendrick enjoys in the town?"

"Oh I'm quite aware of that. Local Mayor I believe. Well, sounds like he's a man with a sound enough reputation. Conscientious type I'd say, from first impressions at least. I'll know more when I start to report to him."

"Well sir," replied Megan, "I was hoping you could do me a small favour. I've greatly respected Mr. Hendrick for some time now and would dearly like to meet him just once. Do you think I could visit the mill tomorrow and, if so, what time would Mr. Hendrick be receptive?"

"Oh, you'd like me to introduce you then?" said Ferguson. "Well it's all a bit soon, don't you think? Tomorrow *is* my very first day. Let me see. He's got a visit from the Monamolin hay-dealers early. But what of that? They'll be on the road again by noon. Tell you what. Why don't you call to the mill at two o'clock. Ask for myself and I'll take you to Mr. Hendrick's office there and then, assuming he's not otherwise engaged at the time. How does that suit?"

"You're very kind," replied the young woman in an appreciative tone. "Tell Mr. Hendrick that a young lady wishes to speak to him about a distant relative of his who has recently arrived in Castlebridge."

"Ah, family matters. Well from the little I know of Michael I'm sure he'll be well disposed to speak with you. See you at two o'clock then. Good night for now, and thanks for supper."

"Good night."

With that Megan-Leanne descended the stairs once more, collected her and her mother's supper things, and repaired to their room. To suggest that Megan's news of her pre-arranged meeting with the Mayor was well received by her mother would have been putting it mildly. Susanna Redmond immediately began to rehearse with her daughter how the latter should approach this encounter, which was at that time still some fifteen hours off. She instructed her daughter to speak kindly to the Mayor and, at the appropriate time, to name the name of 'Susanna Redmond widow of Nicky Redmond, a sailor'. She was then to ask Mr. Hendrick if he wished to meet this distant relative and, if so, to name a designated time and place for it. Megan concurred and the two women, tired from their hectic day, resolved to sleep on the matter. The details could be fine-tuned over breakfast.

Mother and daughter finished their supper. Megan then conveyed their empty supper-tray down the staircase and on into the kitchen where their beneficent hosts were tidying up for the night. On her return she sauntered briefly into the bar area only to find Robert Ferguson enjoying a late pint with two of the locals. She instantly recognised the two as men she had spoken to earlier in the day, namely Simon Lowney and Christy Colfer. She also noted with amusement that, as far as sampling the local brew was concerned, both men seemed to have had something of a head-start on the Dubliner.

With slurred speech and raised voices they pontificated on how this new man should supplant 'that scoundrel Hendrick' as chief barley merchant, if not as Mayor! Mildly amused by this discourse Megan-Leanne chuckled to herself, mounted the staircase and retired for the night.

CHAPTER 6

❦

Family Matters

The next morning dawned bright and crisp as any September morning could. As Susanna Redmond drew the curtains the low autumn sun streamed into their room with a luminosity that was dazzling to both. It was some minutes short of eight o'clock and, peering down on the street below, both women noticed that a guest had just walked out of the inn. As he exited Megan perceived it to be none other than Robert Ferguson. He strolled up the street whistling to himself, crossed the canal bridge, turned to his right and directed his footsteps towards the mill.

As Mrs. Redmond and her daughter took breakfast in the common room of their tavern, trepidation sat on the face of the elder woman. Megan was cooperative in all respects and for her own part could perceive no sound reason why this man would decline her mother's invitation.

"But what if he does answer 'No'?" she enquired of her mother.

"If he declines," replied Mrs. Redmond, "you should be civil, thank him for his time, tell him we wish him well in his business, and then inform him that we will both leave Castlebridge at our earliest convenience."

Later that morning Susanna Redmond and her daughter departed The Pikeman's Inn, but not before they had spent some time making Megan respectable. At length, the clock struck two. Now was the allotted hour for the young girl to present herself at the mill. Her mother then caringly adjusted her daughter's bonnet, took her by the hand, kissed her and wished her well.

Business in the town was energetic as ever. On her short walk to the mill Megan-Leanne was served not a few reminders of the local commercial importance of the relative she would presently meet. Several carriage vans lined the narrow streets of Castlebridge. Most of these had hailed from Wexford Town or from the nearby villages of Curracloe, Blackwater, Redgate, Skreen, Crossabeg and Oylegate to name but a few. Megan noted with interest that the loads of hay, barley, wheat and oats that burdened these carriages almost without exception bore the inscription

"Hendrick—Miller, Merchant and Barley Dealer".

Approaching the entrance to the milling complex and curiously regarding all that was being transacted both without and within its confines, Megan-Leanne Redmond knew full well she stood on territory that was altogether unfamiliar. The girl's own childhood memories, almost without exception, centred on the town of New Ross. There she had observed much that was marine; how sailors, fishmongers and shipwrights had earned their livelihood, and how emigrants had set sail for England, France and other lands. She had, as has already been remarked, spent the last three years in one far distant land but again the family had settled at a fishing port. Castlebridge was an altogether different proposition. Here the flourishing of the town depended solely on the success of all matters arable. Trusses of hay (as well as copious quantities of oats, malt and barley) were busily conducted hither and thither at the mill.

Attempting to feign some degree of acquaintance with such surroundings Megan-Leanne confidently passed under the archway that stood beside the huge millwheel and began to search for Mr. Ferguson. It did not take long. Through one of the quaint round windows in the stone building to her left she could recognise the man inside as none other than the mill's newly appointed barleycorn manager, Mr. Robert Ferguson. She knocked gently on the door, was cordially invited in, and duly entered the office. The young Kingstown man was barely half-a-day in this new position and had just returned from lunch. This he had taken in one of the six public houses the town boasted in those days. He stood behind a large wooden table that seemed to have several small bags of grain on it, some of which were open and partially spilled. Megan stood facing him from the opposite side of the table.

"Ah," the young man cried, "you're as good as your word young maiden. Mr. Hendrick is expecting you, though he may be a few minutes. He's got some unfinished business you might say." At this he glanced towards the door to Hendrick's office, lowered his voice, leaned over the table and whispered to Megan "trouble with the staff."

The girl nodded demurely. Then Ferguson pulled up a chair and bade her be seated. Shutting out from one's consciousness the raised voices and heated tones coming from the adjoining office would have required considerably more effort of will than overhearing them.

From what could be gleaned a man called Jacob, who had given years of service to Mr. Hendrick and was widely tipped as being the eventual appointee to the position recently advertised, was indignant at that same position being filled by a stranger or, to use Jacob's own phrase, a 'blow-in'. The fact that this new man had no record at the mill was unpalatable enough, but he was not even from Castlebridge. Indeed Jacob detected instantly from the young man's accent that he was not even likely to be from the county. Hendrick rebutted the accusations and, thumping his hand hard on the table to signify his limited patience with Jacob, insisted in a voice yet more voluminous that he retains his right to appoint staff solely on the basis of merit.

"My men earn their crust by provin' their worth," he contended. "If one o' my men shows he's not up to the job then it's out the door with him, yella-belly or no. Take that Amos Wickham now. He'll get his final warnin' one o' these days, turnin' up for work a full forty minutes late. What does he mean by it? Bein' born and bred in Castlebridge won't save him if he keeps that up. You watch me. And another thing, I expect all my men to work as a team. Be sure of it Jacob, I'll be takin' a dim view of any hard words I overhear between yerself and Ferguson. But yel find he's an agreeable sort o' fella, punctual and with a good work rate."

Incandescent with rage Jacob pursed his lips, sighed audibly, turned towards the door and exited, slamming it hard. On his way through the outer office he may have minded to direct some sneering remark to his new colleague had he not deemed as rather uncouth such utterances in the presence of a lady. Megan-Leanne found that her mind had been sidetracked by the general mood in the office. Now she needed to gather her thoughts once more ahead of what might be a delicate interview with the Mayor. Judging from the relative disdain with which Michael Hendrick had addressed one of his workers, and a long-serving one at that, she mused over whether such circumstances might afford a favourable occasion for the discussion of family matters. Just then Robert Ferguson winked at Megan, signalled to her to stand, and then entered Hendrick's office.

"Eh, it's that young girl I told you about this morning," he said. "You remember, who wanted to see you about some long-lost relative or something? I never caught her name though."

"Oh yes, yes," replied Hendrick without even raising his head, "that's alright, send her in. I'm ready, and she'll not be as hard on me as Jacob, eh?"

Ferguson then beckoned the young woman to the door, the latter signifying her gratitude with a faint smile.

"Well, why don't I leave you two to get acquainted? I'll just get back to my grain," said Ferguson gently closing the door and returning to the outer office.

Hendrick raised his glance toward the young maiden who now stood in his office. Her fair face with its elegant contours wore an unassuming expression just then. Hendrick noticed how her large round eyes were fixed intently on him. Her gait as she entered the office, along with the pleasurable aura this young woman seemed to carry around with her, were in marked contrast to the gruff rawness of the man with whom he had just engaged. *He* had left in a fit of pique, *she* had arrived with a tangible air of agreeability. *His* manner was one of resentment at the world's disappointments, *hers* one of serenity in spite of them. Hendrick, though reputed for his candid nature, spoke to the young woman in moderate tones.

"Afternoon, young maiden. And how may I be of assistance?" he asked wearing a mildly hospitable expression.

"Mr. Hendrick sir, can I speak with you a few minutes? It's family, not business, and I'll not take up too much of your time. You seem busy today."

"Ah, things are always busy at the mill. But thank God, eh. And now I've my new man some o' the pressure's off. What is it, young girl, that yeh wish to tell me?"

"I've been sent to inform you that a distant relative of yours, one Susanna Redmond the widow of mariner Nicky Redmond, is at present staying in Castlebridge and wishes to learn whether you will meet with her or no."

Hendrick's face, which hitherto had worn an expression of indifference, now displayed one of positive kindliness, even compassion. He took the girl by the hand and then, with a gentleness even he had forgotten he was capable of, lowered her softly into a chair. He then pulled up his own chair so that it stood next to hers. Sitting down and taking her hand once more, he spoke to her tenderly.

"Would you, by any chance, be the daughter of this Susanna Redmond?" he enquired.

"Yes sir. Her only daughter, in fact."

"And what do they call you?"

"Megan is my name, sir. Megan-Leanne Redmond."

"I see," said the Mayor closing his eyes and tightening his grip on the girl's hand. Then he released it again, stood up and walked towards the window of his office. There he stood with his back to his visitor. At the very moment that the pretty young maid had uttered the words 'Megan is my name', Hendrick's eyes had suffused with tears and he wished to compose himself before proceeding.

Some moments later he walked to the door and called to his foreman to fetch tea and cakes for the visitor. Ferguson complied at once. The Mayor seemed greatly interested in everything Megan had to say. After some time he ventured to ask the girl how long her mother had been widowed.

"We only lost father last month," was Megan's reply.

Hendrick stirred visibly on every occasion that the word 'father' was used to refer to the sailor. His mind was taken right back to Wellingtonbridge all those eighteen years ago. Considering his fruitless return to the fair in her pursuit, Hendrick marvelled that his wife was still alive—and was living in Ireland.

"Yeh mentioned that yeh were raised in New Ross, am I right?"

"Yes, though about three years ago father's work took us to Canada and it was there that we lost him. His vessel got into difficulties off the coast of Greenland and the crew were reported drowned."

"Indeed, indeed. Now tell me dear, is yer mother in good health?"

"She's tired, weary and spent out. It's all the travelling."

"And where's she stayin' in Castlebridge just now?"

"We're staying at The Pikeman's Inn. I'm sure you know it, just at the bottom of town."

"I know it well. Many of my men frequent the place. As for me, I don't touch the bottle these days but I know good aul' Stafford and his wife, daycent skins the pair o' them. If I were to write a short note to yer mother just now, could yeh take it to her discreetly?"

"With pleasure," replied Megan innocently.

"And in confidence?"

"Of course."

Taking his pen and paper, Michael Hendrick set about writing a short note to 'Mrs. Susanna Redmond'. It's wording was as follows:

> *"You're alive against all odds. I thank Heaven for it. The maiden has related to me the loss of Redmond, yet seems altogether unacquainted*

with the truth. It's well you keep it from her still, at least until we've met. Meet me at The Bogside at eight tonight. See you then,

—M. Hendrick."

He folded the paper, directed it, sealed it and handed it to Megan-Leanne. Taking her once more by the hand he raised her to her feet and, with a gentle smile, wished her good afternoon. When Megan-Leanne had departed, Hendrick marvelled at how kind fate could at times be. Just days earlier he was short of the barleycorn manager his business so urgently required, and up to that very afternoon he had believed that his wife Susanna had been long in her grave. Now, Ferguson was busily making a success of the barley end of the business and Susanna was alive against the odds.

The Mayor's house was located on the outskirts of Castlebridge. Susanna and her daughter had in their innocence walked in full view of it that very week on entering the town for the first time. It was located on Codd's Walk, a thoroughfare of which mention has already been made. On leaving Castlebridge to travel westward it was not difficult to ascertain the precise point at which one was to leave the town proper and thence set foot on the byways and dust-trails of the county. On arriving at Codd's Bridge one was confronted by a fork in the road. The road veering right lead one to the rustic town-lands of Crory, Randallsmill, Monroe, Castlesow, Tobberfinnick and, a little further, Redgate. The Crossabeg road to the left—the one that was evidently the more travelled—lead to Fairyhill, Artramon, St. Edmond's and, ultimately, to Kyle Cross, a junction with one of the most important thoroughfares in the county. As it proceeded south past an area known as The Bogside, the tributary that flowed out from under Codd's Bridge not only formed the boundary between Castlebridge and the surrounding area but also delineated the borders of Hendrick's own estate.

The house itself was a large construction on a generous plot. Any visitor to Castlebridge would have been left in little doubt that its owner was a man or woman of no small means. But it was built on sloped land so that its inhabitants were afforded a commanding view of any pedestrians crossing the bridge below. Yet, those very pedestrians enjoyed an equally comprehensive aspect on all that took place in the back garden of the same estate, many stalling to admire how the Mayor's well tended lawn scarped gracefully down to the stream's bank. Hendrick was eager that, so as not to unnecessarily arouse any suspicions, Susanna would not be seen entering his house. He had arranged to meet her at The Bogside, in an area about half way between Hendrick's own estate and the top of Main Street. This was a location that was easy to find but also afforded discretion. It was thence that Hendrick conducted his wife. They entered the house through its side-entrance and then sat down in its spacious kitchen.

"Well Susanna," he said nervously, "nobody knows we're here. Nobody, that is, except our daughter Megan. And before yeh say anythin' let me tell yeh that I'm off the drink. In fact I'm after takin' a vow and I've not touched the stuff since that very night."

Susanna sat motionless, staring out of the kitchen window. She barely had the physical strength or strength of will to stand and confront her long-lost husband face to face. The Mayor continued in conciliatory tones.

"Not knowin' whether yerself or the child were alive or dead I returned to Wellingtonbridge the followin' autumn and left message with that auld hag. I had hoped that yed come back sooner. But seein' as how yeh didn't I forsook the chase after a year or two. This mornin' I learnt from Megan that the sailor was lost, somethin' about a shippin' accident near Greenland or somethin', and figured that was why yed sought me. Was that it Susanna? Had yeh resolved to be faithful to Redmond until death do ye part?"

"I had Michael and I believe I'm right in it. That man paid a handsome price for me and I felt bound to him for it. Besides, he treated both of us, myself and my daughter, as befits a respectable husband and father."

Hendrick winced. Though she had not stated it he understood, by omission, that his own reputation was in sharp contrast. He was clearly all that a husband and father should *not* be, or at least ought not to have been those many years ago. They discussed their options and, at length, concurred on the most appropriate course open to them. They would arrange a religious ceremony in some remote part of the county, a ceremony at which only Megan-Leanne and a second witness would be the guests. They would also need to arrange an impostor who would purport to represent the registrar. All this was to satisfy Megan-Leanne as to the propriety of the situation. All three would then take up residence in Hendrick's house, Megan continuing to believe that the Mayor was her stepfather and that her mother had simply married this distant relative as any widow was free to do. Hendrick suggested that they both take some days to consider the finer details of it, and then make a definite decision by the following week.

"I'm told y'are stayin' at The Pikeman's Inn?"

"That's right. It will do for now. We help out a little in the chores. You know how it is?"

"Aye, aye. Yeh should stay there for the time bein' until such time as things are more definite. Y'are in good hands with aul' Stafford and I'll furnish yeh with whatever means is required in the interim. Here, take this for now and don't be short of anythin'."

He handed her an envelope. She opened it, peered inside and counted its contents. There was a Bank of Ireland £1 note, an Hibernian Bank £3 note and four half-crowns. The amount was significant, but not because it was liberal—and liberal it certainly was—but for a far more poignant reason that was not lost on Susanna. She felt as though the Mayor was attempting to buy her back again after all these years. Staring into the envelope, she fingered the money thoughtfully.

Sentimentality taught her that this must be the exact set of notes and coins Redmond had paid for her those eighteen years previously. Had she taken the trouble to examine the money in any detail, she would have hastily dismissed such a fantasy. Only two of the coins showed hallmarks of age. These were dusky brown in hue and their embossments were so worn down with decades of use that one could barely discern the flamboyant, curly tresses of the long-dead George the Second. In sharp contrast, the other two shone with all the glistening clarity of coins freshly minted and lucidly portrayed the rugged, weather-beaten profile of the recently crowned William the Fourth. What's more, Hibernian had only been printing its own banknotes (or 'tokens') a mere six years. But Susanna Redmond was a woman of simple intellect and all such subtleties were outside the scope of her perception.

Then, as though his timing was quite deliberate, Hendrick chose this moment to make a proposal. It was one to which he was nervously unsure how his wife might react.

"If we go ahead with this our plan, to meet as if by chance, then to court, then to marry, and Megan-Leanne comes to live with us in this very house, wouldn't it be the desired thing for Megan to adopt my surname?"

"No, no, not at all!" cried Susanna with surprising alacrity. "You know how fine a line we're treading here Michael. We must at all costs keep the truth from her, poor innocent maiden that she is. If I'm to marry you as the widow of Redmond, Megan being my daughter, then she should remain a Redmond even when I take your name."

"Oh well," replied the Mayor resignedly, "just seems a little daft don't yeh think, when Mr. and Mrs. *Hendrick* introduce their young girl as Megan-Leanne *Redmond*? I'll get used to it no doubt."

"Be that as it may, I'd rather strangers be puzzled at our circumstances than for Megan to learn the full truth. We must keep her in ignorance on it, Michael. We absolutely must. How would she respond if we revealed all? Eh? Would she not revile us both? I'm lonely in the world, Michael, and in failing health just now. How could I survive my own daughter's vilification? Her implied and affectionate trust in her mother would evaporate in an instant. She'd have as much disdain for you Michael, bein' the one who started the matter. Any pressure to change her surname might run the risk of kindling suspicion if we appear too keen on it. Besides, she's a sweet young maiden upon whom many eyes have already turned in Castlebridge. She'll scarcely bring the sailor's name to her grave don't you think?"

"Well, that's very true. It's just a male thing I suppose. My own daughter, my very own flesh and blood, comes to live with me and bears the name of a stranger, and a dead one at that. Anyway y'are probably right. Discretion is the better part of valour. We'll say no more on't."

With that they parted. Hendrick knew it would be foolish to offer to accompany Susanna any part of the journey back to her lodging. He wished her well, they ventured to shake hands, and she departed.

CHAPTER 7

❃

Sound Advice

The next day was a Thursday and Robert Ferguson's second full day at the mill. Just before midday Hendrick approached his recently appointed barleycorn manager and, with a genial smile, made him an invitation.

"Y'are not a wet day in the place Ferguson and already yer skills have made no small impression. Y'are reliable and punctual. Y'are cordial too, and honest. Yeh seem like a man I could depend on and, Ferguson, the type o' man I could confide in. Let me treat yeh to yer dinner tonight. There's no shortage of places to eat in the town but they do a quare good platter at The South Leinster Arms. Why don't yeh join me, eh?"

"You say you're impressed with my work. But I'm only here a day and you're liberal in your rewards. But what's this about 'confiding'? Is there something on your mind, something you wish to discuss maybe? Is that what it's all about?"

"Well, I'll be honest yes. Yeh see Robert, I might be liked about the town. I might be head of this great business and be Mayor and all the rest. But I'm one lonely creature, Ferguson. I've lived alone all these long years and I just need some counsel. It's on matters personal if y'understand me."

"Oh well, counsel?" replied Ferguson, "and you want it from a chap nine years your junior?"

Hendrick seized Ferguson's forearm with a grip that was gentle but firm. "Y'are my only friend in the world. Come to dinner and hear my tale."

"I'll not gainsay it," answered Robert. "But you know what season of the year it is Michael. If there's one time for folk in our business to be idle then it's not the harvest. Yet I'll be finished by eight o'clock. I'll see you then, at The South Leinster Arms."

It was with a visible air of expectation that the Mayor of Castlebridge stood waiting for his friend in the lobby of The South Leinster Arms. He'd arrived a full ten minutes early and impatiently removed his timepiece from his breast pocket on several occasions, the interval between each getting shorter as the appointed hour drew near.

Then, as the bell tolled eight Hendrick was joined by the colleague he had now come to regard as a friend and confidant. Ferguson's conscientiousness in completing his several tasks for the day was matched only by his punctuality in meeting with his employer for their pre-arranged dinner. Both men were hungry now and the necessary victuals were ordered. Hendrick acted so as to cause no embarrassment to his manager, yet spared no expense into the bargain. The Mayor addressed his friend amiably.

"Robert," he began, "mine is a long tale and I'll ask yeh to forgive the length of it. But I'm in a quandary and in need of advice."

"Well I'm not in any rush. As for our confidence, none of what's said will out. Take my word on it."

"I do," replied Hendrick confident of his friend's sincerity. "Bein' from Kingstown yel have heard o' summer camps."

"Yes indeed," replied Ferguson. "The thought of it takes me right back to childhood. Ours were typically held in Greystones or somewhere else along the Wicklow coast. I've fond memories of them I can tell you."

"Well so do I, Robert, so do I. But sometimes we'd go beyond Leinster. Wan year, the year I was seventeen and my very last summer at camp, we travelled to Wales. There we stayed in the camp at Ceredigion. I was pleasantly surprised to learn how many Wexford folk had travelled to it that summer, as indeed seemed the case every year, but wan in particular more than any other. She was a little younger than meself and hailed from the village of Adamstown in the west o' the county. Yel know, Ferguson, how high passions can run at seventeen. Well without bein' too graphic, wan thing lead t'another and well I need not tell yeh any more of it. Suffice it to say that I returned from Wales that summer a changed man. Fortunately there was no issue from it so we let matters rest. At that time, she was livin' with some relation or other in the Southern part o' Wales. I'd begun me turnip-snaggin' by then and, though born in Wexford Town, had started to move around the county wherever the trade took me. But it seemed that each time I returned to the family home in Coolcotts a letter awaited me with a Welsh post-mark. The girl came from a wealthy, respectable family and the tone of each letter served to reinforce my fears that such indiscretions as ours were not treated flippantly by members o' polite society. She certainly came from well-to-do stock and well I believed it. She did, however, do us both the favour of remainin' discreet."

At the beginning of this discourse Ferguson's manner was of one who'd expected a tale of some short-changed farmer, or of some tax or other that Hendrick had neglected to pay. When he perceived the direction that the conversation was headed he was at once both uneasy yet fully attentive, and the Mayor could read this readily from his friend's expressions just then.

"In the followin' spring, the spring of eighteen-eleven, I received a letter from her that caused my entire bein' to shudder. She explained that she was soon to reach legal marriage age and that—"

"*What?*" gasped Ferguson, leaning forward. You mean she—"

"*Don't,* Ferguson!" interrupted Hendrick raising his hand to the man.

The Mayor acted as though he almost expected this interjection, and even then Ferguson was not entirely convinced of what it was that had caused Hendrick to shudder. Was it the girl's suggestion of marriage itself or was it the revelation of her being below a certain age? He fancied rather that it was most likely a combination of the two. As far as Hendrick was concerned it was a mere exchange of intimacies between two young adults in a moment of passion. Robert Ferguson leant back in his chair and beckoned the Mayor to continue.

"The followin' year my work took me to the north o' the county. Well that very winter, at a Christmas dance in Courtown, I met another young maiden. She was the wan age o' me mind yeh and went by the name o' Susanna Mac-Murrough. She was from Carrick-on-Bannow, a village in the south, and was on holidays with family and friends. Not bein' a man who learns a lesson easily and bein' a drinker at the time, I allowed meself to slip again. I mentioned that there was no issue from the encounter in Wales. Well this time I was not so fortunate."

Ferguson was all but entranced by these revelations. Here was he, a visitor from cosmopolitan Kingstown, listening to the respected Mayor of a rural town uncovering the sordid details of his teenage exploits. Hendrick went on to relate his marriage to Susanna at Ferns the following spring and how they'd settled at Taghmon, where Megan-Leanne was born in the autumn. He told of how his work had once again taken him to different parts of the county and how, when Megan was just one, they had ended up at Wellingtonbridge. Ferguson was utterly astounded by the story of the auction but by now was prepared to believe anything of this man, or nothing.

"Now yeh must understand, Robert, that when the first girl caught wind o' my marriage to Susanna she all but gave up on her quest and, to my lastin' relief, the letters ceased. It's an ill wind, eh? But four year ago, at th'age o' thirty-five, I was elected Mayor o' Castlebridge for the first time. Naturally, I was honoured to serve in this capacity and knew it would be well publicised. Two things I was ignorant of however. Wan was that our local newspaper would mention that the town's new Mayor was a single man, and th'other that copies o' The Castle & Bridge would make their way across the water."

Ferguson smiled subtly at the unintended pun, and then gestured to the Mayor to continue.

"Learnin' o' my state, and not bein' wed herself, the dogged young maid lost no time in resumin' her correspondence. Like meself, she had assumed that Susanna was dead and that I was once again free to marry. I let the matter rest and didn't respond, hopin' she'd assume my family had sold up Coolcotts and left no forwardin' address. But when I was re-elected Mayor two year ago, the letters started arrivin' here. All were addressed to 'Mayor Hendrick, Town Hall, Castlebridge, Co. Wexford.' I could no longer plead ignorance and responded sayin' I was not long widowed and the whole business would take some gettin' used to. The letters continued to flood in, now with an alarmin' frequency, and each more candid than the last. She recounted every last detail of our night on the beach in Wales. How and where it had happened, what we'd both been wearin', how long it had lasted and so on. She desperately pleaded with me to marry her, as if her marryin' someone else would be to somehow rob him o' somethin' he had a right t'expect. Then finally, this very summer, I was elected Mayor for the third and final time. In her letter o' congratulations, she remarked that I was now widowed for at least four years. She asked if she returned to Wexford and came to Castlebridge would I marry her. To be honest with yeh Ferguson, I saw no reason to decline. By now Susanna was long gone and I scarcely expected to see either herself or me daughter ever again. I wrote to Wales and accepted. The woman was overwhelmed with excitement. In the next letter, which arrived just the wan month ago, she informed me that she'd begun to make arrangements. Leavin' Wales for good and returnin' t'Ireland would take some preparation but she expected to be settled in Castlebridge within a year. No sooner was the course set but who turns up only

Susanna. Not only that, but she's after bringin' the maiden with her. I met Susanna privately last night and we agreed that our best course was to fake our weddin' in some remote parish o' the county. Then herself and Megan could come and live in my house on Codd's Walk. But yeh can see, Robert, what a quandary I'm in now. I must act soon. I'm goin' t'ave to shatter the dreams o' wan o' these two women. Which'll it be?"

By now Ferguson had buried his head in his hands and was almost at a loss for words. Just then he raised his head while leaving his hands in their cupping position. "You know full well which one of these women you must disappoint. You're only asking my advice to satisfy your own conscience on it. That night in Wales was, what, twenty-two years ago? It was a brief moment of fervour for you both. There was no commitment to marry in it, implied or otherwise. You'll have to decline her offer Michael."

Hendrick leaned back in his chair contemplating this remarkable man for some moments. He had come to hold his foreman in an esteem that bordered on veneration. He perceived him to be a man of good moral repute in his own dealings, yet there was something of an independent spirit in Robert that the Mayor couldn't help but admire. Received values were not above scrutiny. Those that were proven to be helpful ought to be adhered to, yet none should be naïvely complied with in blind obedience. He seemed to contend that such precepts were given for mankind's benefit and, like the Sabbath that was made for man, ought only to be embraced to the extent that they well served the folks involved. There was something refreshing, indeed liberating, in Robert Ferguson's heterodox approach to these matters. He was not a man of facile or shallow intellect.

But challenging the conventional values of the day would have brought either man into sharp disagreement with the local clergy in Castlebridge, as indeed it would have done in Kingstown. Besides all this Hendrick, unlike Ferguson, was the local Mayor. He knew full well that on such delicate matters he could not but proceed with extreme caution.

"Well my instinct is y'are right," admitted Hendrick. "I'm already married to Susanna. As long as she's alive, I'll remain so."

"Oh indeed," responded Ferguson. "And you're right in saying you must act promptly. It must be perceived in the town that you are the undisputed husband of Susanna, in good time for the return of the first girl. It's mid-September now so you'll need to arrange that ceremony soon. But the Mayor of Castlebridge should be married in Castlebridge and not outside. I think it's unwise to arouse your daughter's suspicion unnecessarily. Let it all be above board. I'll help out in any way I can. You mentioned you needed a second witness? Well count me in for that anyway."

"It's probably too late to dissuade th'other woman from comin' to Castlebridge," said Hendrick solemnly. "But I'll not have her turnin' up in the town to be greeted by the news. It's best she learns of it in advance. So I'll write to her soon, leavin' her in no doubt that I'm already a married man. Yet I'll do what I can to keep matters civil between us when she arrives, as it looks certain she will. If it doesn't change her mind, so be it. I'll suffer to live in the same town as her. I'm only Mayor for another two years at any rate."

"That's as best Michael," came Ferguson's reply. "Don't keep her in the dark."

With that, the two men shook hands and parted.

CHAPTER 8

Trouble at Mill

Some two weeks or so had passed since the wedding day and the new family was settling in at Michael Hendrick's large house on Codd's Walk. One morning, as the three sat for breakfast the Mayor noticed that his wife looked a good deal paler than she had done for some considerable time. That Susanna had lost weight there could be no doubt and her face owned a sunken, even gaunt appearance that neither he nor Megan had noticed before.

Hendrick regarded her keenly over the breakfast table. He then recollected some words that he'd overheard at the wedding reception in The South Leinster Arms. The words were spoken by Nancy Muckridge and, though he could not recall them verbatim, seemed to suggest that Susanna Redmond was a weak-willed woman of failing strength and limited means. Before the wedding day itself Hendrick had been aware of the several slights that were being put upon Susanna. There was consternation at the Mayor's seeming to marry so comparatively beneath himself. He was a well-built and vigorous man of means. She was slight of frame, unassertive and meagre in pocket. He had hoped that life would improve when she finally found some stability. Yet he noted with increasing concern that Susanna's health seemed to be deteriorating daily.

It was now early November and the total daylight was visibly shortening by the day. In order to avail of what few lighted hours there were Hendrick's men were each under instruction to report for duty no later than half past seven. This enabled deliveries to commence at first light.

One morning, Ferguson arrived at his office promptly. It was in fact closer to seven that to half past but Ferguson fancied he would light his fire and brew some tea before the rigours of the day began. He walked past the mill wheel, turned left under the archway and proceeded up the courtyard towards his office. On arriving, he noticed that the door was double-locked and, in spite of scant light, could also perceive some kind of rugged object, perhaps an old plank of wood, wedged under the door. Now it must be pointed out that security at the mill was not a subject for mere academic discussion. Men like Hendrick and Ferguson were all too conscious of likely pilferers that lurked, should they fail in the task. What puzzled the young man, however, was that such security was typically designed to keep intruders *out*. Why this seemingly deliberate attempt to keep someone *in*?

As Ferguson suspected that something untoward had happened he resolved in his mind to enquire about the matter of Hendrick when the two met later that morning. He then removed the plank, unlocked the door, and entered the office. Everything seemed to be pretty much as he expected. Lighting his candle he could see how his desk was laid out as he had left it the evening before, how his many ledgers sat in orderly fashion on their respective shelves, and how his bags of grain were stacked neatly in a corner. Yes, everything seemed in its rightful place. Nothing was missing, nothing was added, and nothing was moved. There was bound to be a perfectly rational explanation for the wedge.

He glanced around once more, shrugged his shoulders and then removed his great coat. Conducting himself towards the fire hearth at the chimney end of the office, Ferguson suddenly noticed a rather large object wrapped in straggly clothes and sprawled out before the fireplace. On drawing his candle closer to the bundle, he noticed several slices of orange-peel strewn around the floor in its vicinity. But these afforded no clue. With some trepidation Ferguson advanced towards the object, pulled away some of the rags and instantly recognised the face as that of Amos Wickham, one of Hendrick's drivers.

"Amos Wickham! Good heavens!" exclaimed Ferguson, but Wickham did not stir. "What in the name of," continued the manager, noting with relief that steam passed out from under the youth's nostrils.

Conscious of how icy a morning it was, Ferguson kindled his fire with all manner of haste. He then began to shake this young Amos Wickham character out of his deep slumber. It took some effort yet within a minute or so Wickham was awake. But the manner of his waking propelled the young man into a lather that was to Ferguson bemusing, disturbing and very nearly frightening. Wickham was a youth of barely sixteen years. He had an annoying tendency to take rather short breaths while conducting any kind of interchange with those he regarded as his seniors. His skin, which was unwholesomely deficient in the natural tinge, was barely visible under his straggled curly brown hair. All that could be seen clearly in the dim light were two large and quivering purple lips that spluttered as he spoke.

"What time is it Mr. Ferguson? Eh, have I slept it out? Eh, I mean, does Mr. Hendrick know? Eh, should I be on the road by now, what time is it? I have to get goin' don't I?"

"Pull yourself together and calm down," remonstrated Ferguson, irritated by the youth's maladroitness. "What sort of thing is going on here? Haven't you got a home to go to? What's all this antic of sleeping in the office like some kind of vagabond, eh? What's it all about? Now out with it."

"It's Mr. Hendrick sir, it's all his doin'."

"What do you mean, Wickham? What on earth do you mean? What about Mr. Hendrick?"

"Well sir," continued the lad in a tremulous voice, "yeh know how I do find it hard, yeh know, to be wakin' up i' the mornin', and how I've been late this last while, what with these dark mornin's and no larks and all? Well I turned up late again yesterda' and Mr. Hendrick was bullin' with rage. Oh, he chased me 'round the courtyard last night, sir. He said I needed teachin' a lesson so he locked me in here for the night, said it was th'only way o' makin' sure I was at work at half seven. 'Twas terrible cold last night sir, that's why I slept at the fire. I took some o' yer logs from the scuttle. I hope yel not mind, but I thought I'd catch me death. And I was quare hungry too. I'm after takin' an oarnge from yer locker. I seen two there but I took only the wan. It's that oarnge that's kept me alive, Mr. Ferguson. I don't know what me poor father'll say, he must o' thought somethin' terrible had happened with me not comin' home yester evenin'."

"Never mind your father. I'd love to know what Constable Burke will say if it's ever reported."

Wickham stared at Ferguson for some moments, the intense uneasiness still evident in the former's demeanour. As for Ferguson, he was horrified by what seemed to have taken place.

"Listen to me Wickham," he said grabbing the youth by both his elbows and straightening him up. "You run off back home now to your cottage, get yourself tidied up, grab a quick bite to eat, tell your Dad you'll explain later, and be back here for a quarter to eight. I make that about twenty-five minutes in all. Now is that fair?"

"But sir, a load's gotta be in Blackwater by half past eight, another in Riverchapel by noon. Eh, and after that there's—"

"*Wickham!*" interrupted Ferguson raising his voice, "I'll not send you to Blackwater, to Riverchapel or anywhere else the state you're in. Now get off with you!"

"But what if *he* catches—"

"Leave Mr. Hendrick to me. You just be here at a quarter to."

A faint smile appeared on Amos Wickham's face. Then he flew out of the office, tore down the courtyard and out under the archway. But he'd not gone far when he was jolted by a large sturdy hand that grabbed him by the scruff of his neck.

"And where might *you* be off to, Amos Wickham?" demanded an all too familiar voice. It was, as the lad had feared, that of Mr. Michael Hendrick.

"I'm just, eh, well sir, I'm just off—"

"Well, out with it! Where?"

"Mr. Ferguson sent me sir. Yeh see sir, he said I could pop home for a bit sir, just twenty minutes or so, nottin' more, just so I could freshen up a little and, eh, I could get a morsel or two sir, just before we start out for the day. I'll not be long."

Hendrick then repositioned his hand away from Wickham's neck and onto his large head of curly hair. Unable to conquer his instinctive propensity to berate his men for their weaknesses, he dragged the boy back into the courtyard and stood him outside the window of Ferguson's office. That Wickham was in agony was obvious, though he desisted from complaining just then for fear of the Mayor. Ferguson stormed out of his office in horror at the sight.

"Now yeh see this Ferguson? This is how yeh teach a man a lesson, how yeh drum bein' on time into him." The Mayor then took hold of Wickham's left ear, turned it so that the youth's face was twisted with pain, and said in a loud voice, "Get out from this courtyard, get into them stirrups and off to Blackwater with yeh. When y'are finished there yeh know there's a load for Riverchapel at twelve and we've got a collection from Newtownbarry at three."

"*Newtownbarry?*" screamed Wickham. "That's almost in the next county. If I'm to be there for three and home before sundown, when'll I get ten minutes for a bit o' dinner? I mean I'll be on the road all day with these—"

"Shut that gob o' yours Wickham!" shouted Hendrick in vituperative tones, "and mother o'Gad if yeh don't make them calls today or yeh show up late once more, it's roasted alive I'll be havin' yeh for breakfast, dinner and tay. Now get to it."

Hendrick released his grip, but as Wickham began to scurry away his boss reached forward and kicked the driver with such force that he skidded and then fell forward on the gravel. When he stood up the imprint of the Mayor's boot was evident on the young man's britches and he stumbled back down under the archway towards his horse and wagon.

Ferguson stood in the courtyard wearing an expression of grave indignation. He was aghast at what he had just witnessed. He wondered if there was any depth to which this belligerent man would not stoop. As Wickham's horse was about to depart Ferguson called to him and threw two large red apples in his direction. Wickham caught the apples gratefully. Then drawing his breath and confronting the Mayor, the barleycorn manager spoke directly to him.

"Michael," he cried admonishingly, "We no longer treat servants in this manner, no less our workmen. It's not proper. And besides, a time will come and is perhaps not far off when the workers will not stand for this kind of thing. They'll start to organise among themselves Michael. You've probably heard of all the troubles at Tolpuddle where—"

"I've a business to run, Ferguson. I'm not interested in rumours o' some West Country village with a strange name. It's entirely a matter for th'English. That young man'll be on time for work tomorra. Yeh better believe it."

"That's only because he's scared out of his wits by *you*," expostulated Ferguson.

"So be it," replied the Mayor sententiously. "If workin' for me don't suit him, he can drive for someone else."

"You know he can't Michael. He can only work in Castlebridge, what with his penniless father and that young sister of his that can't walk."

Hendrick paused. These words had seemed to strike with some little discord on his ear.

"I never knew," he said almost whispering, "that Wickham had a crippled sister!"

"Perhaps you never asked," retorted Ferguson assertively. "At any rate, I'll not be manager in a business where this sort of thing goes on. It's despotic of you Michael. You ought to be ashamed of yourself. If you want me to continue as manger of the barleycorn department, or in any position at this mill, you're going to have to put a stop to it all and treat the men *like* men."

"Then it seems, Mr. Ferguson," answered Hendrick, "that we'll not be workin' together after all. Yeh may leave my service this very day."

Ferguson looked disdainfully at his employer, then grabbed his few things and walked out from under the arch. Hendrick suffered from a self-combating proclivity to antagonise his employees on the slightest provocation. Today, Wickham had overstepped the mark and had been duly punished. But Hendrick's zeal to exact that punishment had cost him his foreman. He suffered now for his own brutish instinct and determined obstinacy. Tension permeated every corner of the courtyard as the labourers all stared at the scene in disbelief. Hendrick addressed them gruffly.

"What are y'all starin' at, eh?" he demanded in a loud, peremptory, voice. "Haven't yeh work to do?"

CHAPTER 9

The Truth Revealed

By the following summer, Robert Ferguson had endeavoured to establish his own barley dealing business. This enterprise was by now trading in rivalry with Hendrick's and already drawing away much of the latter's custom. Yet this was not the Mayor's greatest concern in that sultry summer of eighteen thirty-three. For by this time his wife Susanna was totally bedridden. Her condition was irreversible. The family well knew that, never having been a woman of great physical fortitude, she had not many days to spend this side of eternity. Then one Saturday afternoon in early August, Susanna Hendrick's bed was flanked by her husband on its left side and by her daughter on the other.

With an effort of body and will she took one hand of each, held them tight for some seconds, and muttered something barely audible to her husband. From what he could glean it was an appeal to 'see that Megan marries well' or words to that effect. Her vital force slipping away by the second, Susanna Hendrick then slowly turned her face towards her daughter one last time. A faint smile was evident from the older woman, then another firm but gentle squeeze of her daughter's hand, then a last gasping breath, and then silence.

Megan-Leanne leaned over the body of the mother who had loved her so unconditionally (and to whom she herself had been so devoted) and wept bitterly.

If Susanna's health had been deteriorating by the day, then it was equally apparent that Megan-Leanne's comeliness was improving almost by the hour—all this notwithstanding the expression of grief she would wear for some weeks after the loss of her mother and, it must be remarked, closest friend. For this young girl's fine features were of nature's own barns. Nothing could be added to them and nothing taken away. Moreover they were placidly independent of mood, expression, occasion or attire. Some four weeks or so after the funeral fell Megan-Leanne's own birthday. Over breakfast, the Mayor sat staring at the maiden quite bewildered by her stunning good looks.

Evidence that Megan had reached the exquisite bloom of womanhood was irrefutable. If angels ever stooped to dwell in human form, suffering for a season to clothe themselves with mortality, then it might have been contended in Castlebridge that one such seraph had graced the Hendrick household with its delightful presence. The young woman radiated an allure and a charm that were almost beyond depiction. Provocatively plump cherry lips that seemed tailor-made to be kissed, pale cheeks of a delightfully unruffled texture and equable nature, flawlessly symmetric dimples sported whenever a smile or other agreeable expression was being worn, large and startlingly penetrative green eyes that were an enchantment in themselves, eyebrows—slight and delicate both—that sat high and serenely upon the brow like two proximate crescent moons. All these, as well as a thousand other hallmarks of the truly pulchritudinous, sat visibly on the fair countenance of one Megan-Leanne Redmond.

Sad though the death of his wife had been, the Mayor yet believed in his heart that someday in the not too distant future he would have the pleasure of giving his daughter's hand in marriage. He further knew that he would give it to a gentleman, whosoever providence had ordered that to be, who was to be the envy of the town, if not of the barony.

Still passionately concerned that any daughter of his should bare his surname and take it with her either to the altar or the grave, the notion of persuading Megan to legally change her name had once again taken root in his mind. The following January, Hendrick entered his final six months as Town Mayor. His wife was now in her grave some five months, Christmas was behind them and he resolved to finally reveal all to the innocent Megan-Leanne. She had been deceived for far too long and he could bear no more of it. The time had come for the truth to be known.

Then one wintry evening, as the young maiden sat knitting by a large open fire in the spacious living room of Michael Hendrick's house the man himself entered the room and slowly sat down in the chair opposite. Megan's eyes turned briefly up from her work and a faint smile, complete with dimples, appeared on her round face, ruddy as it was from the firelight. He took a deep breath, then leaned forward and spoke to the girl gently.

"Megan my dear, it's time I spoke to yeh on a family matter and wan of great import at that. I've not spoke to yeh about it before and have thought best to leave well alone the matter for a time, what with our great loss in the autumn."

Megan continued to knit, though she could scarcely conceal a distinct look of unease on her visage just then. What had she done? Then maybe she'd done nothing at all. Perhaps Hendrick just wanted her out of the house and working and earning her own keep. What affection, after all, could the man be expected to harbour for a mere stepdaughter? This last thought had especially troubled the girl since Susanna's death. Her mother was now in the next life and beyond hurt, so perhaps Hendrick had only treated her kindly for her mother's sake. With some trepidation she nodded, signalling to the Mayor that he had her attention.

"Megan," he continued in a soft voice, "do yeh think that if I ever had a daughter o' my own, I would treat her with the same consideration as Nicky Redmond treated his?"

"What a question sir," she replied, her eyes still fixed on the knitting. "I'm sure I don't know. You'd love her no doubt, were she your very own. My father really was very kind to us, kind beyond measure. But then you're kind too sir, in your own way. If ever I need new clothes, or need money for something I fancy, then you always provide it. You never quarrel in that way. I only ever have to ask. So yes. If you're that kind to your stepdaughter, then I'll say you're bound to be liberal with your own flesh and blood."

Hendrick stared into the fire. If he were perfectly honest with himself he'd have wished to change the subject there and then, but knew he had set in motion a process he must see—for good or ill—to its conclusion. At any rate to stop now would only serve to postpone the day of revelation. He should seek the final end of a deception that, in his mind, had thoroughly run its course. He took another deep breath and shaded his forehead with one hand thus shielding his view from all but the fire. Then, finally, he broached the delicate subject.

"Megan," he said, "yer mother and I hadn't many secrets, but I'll tell yeh wan yeh should know, and I'll tell yeh here and now. Nicky Redmond was not yer real father."

Though her face was hidden from him just then, he could hear that the knitting had stopped abruptly. He dared not to raise his glance for fear of a look so reproachful that he might be distracted from the form of words he had long rehearsed.

"Permit me to elaborate. Yer mother and I were married many year ago. We did so at Ferns as a young couple. A little later a beautiful daughter was born t'us and when yeh were a babe of barely twelve months, I did a terrible deed that I've regretted ever since. I was fond of an aul' drink or two in them days and too often it got the better o' me. I lost patience with yer mother wan night. It was at the fair in Wellingtonbridge. Not havin' command of my senses I agreed to sell yer good mother and yerself for four pound and ten. It's all true Megan, true as I'm sittin' here. The buyer was a mariner and the mariner's name was Mr. Nicolas Redmond. And so that very night he took yer mother as if his wife. Whether or not we should recognise their union ought not to concern us. Leave that business to Heaven and divine judgement. All that matters now is that yeh know the name and identity of yer true father. He sits opposite yeh Megan. Yer father is the Mayor of Castlebridge."

By this time Megan was in floods of tears, nor was this the puling of some weak and feeble girl. If by her mother's deathbed she had wept bitterly, now the young woman wailed violently. She grasped her knitting tightly in her hand and leaned forward profusely howling her eyes out. Her mother's death was heart-breaking, yet was inevitable. It had long been expected and, in the final days, Megan had come to regard it as a happy release for the woman. Grievous though it was, all the townsfolk had concurred that the event was not a shock. Hendrick's news, in sharp contract, was thrust upon the poor girl like a bolt from the blue.

The combined strain of the sailor's loss, the move to Castlebridge, her mother's re-marriage and the grief for that same woman's death had been enervating enough for the unfortunate girl. Now the culmination of all that grief, together with her own seemingly unfounded fears regarding her future and, finally, this bombshell from the Mayor himself had left the maiden in a state of emotional exhaustion. She continued to bawl profusely. Some minutes later when she had calmed a little, Hendrick resumed.

"Who d'yeh think chose yer Christian name, eh? Didn't I tell yeh fifty times I spent an entire summer in Wales as a lad? Haven't I told yeh 'bout the camp at Ceredigion? Well the woman o' th'house was kind t'every last wan of us. She'd always let us stay up late, playin' games into the small hours and what have yeh. All the lads were fond of her. And it's *her* that y'are named after. Yeh don't think Megan's a Wexford name now, do yeh? I got it in Wales. So now yel understand, my dear daughter, how eager I was t'ave yeh change yer surname.

Yer mother, God rest her, would have executed somethin' called a deed poll all them years ago, doing so on yer behalf. Bein' Mayor and all I'm expected to know about such things. But all that remains for us now is to execute a second, undoin' th'other. There's a pen and some paper on the dresser so, if y'are agreed, I can dictate th'exact wordin' required. When y'are finished we'll both sign it, meself merely as a witness, then I'll take it down to the county office in Wexford Town. Leave the rest of it to me. What's more we'll place an advertisement in The Castle & Bridge so all the townsfolk will know yer proper name, makin' it appear as though y'are still only my stepdaughter. The whole business of it will be accomplished before yeh know it. Well, Megan my dear, are yeh agreed or no?"

"I suppose," whimpered the girl, scarcely able to think, "that if I really am your daughter then I must have your name. It would be the seemly thing to do and the only honourable course open to me."

"Yel not regret it. *Y'are* my daughter and y'are right, it is the proper thing to do. I'll sit over at the table and yeh can join me when y'are ready."

The business took mere minutes. Being a man well learned in such matters, Hendrick could dictate from memory the precise words to be written. They ran thus:

> *"Know all men by these presents which are intended to be enrolled in the Court of King's Bench, Dublin, that I the undersigned Miss Megan-Leanne Hendrick of Slaneyview House, Codd's Walk, Castlebridge, in the Barony of Shelmaliere East, in the County of Wexford, do hereby:—*
>
> 1. *For and on behalf of myself wholly renounce, relinquish and abandon the use of my former surname of Redmond and in place thereof do assume and adopt from the date hereof the surname of Hendrick so that I may hereafter be called known and distinguished not by my former surname of Redmond but by my assumed surname of Hendrick*
>
> 2. *For the purpose of evidencing such change of name as aforesaid I hereby declare that I shall at all times hereafter in all records, deeds and documents and any other writing and in all actions, suits and proceedings as well as in all dealings, transactions matters and things whatsoever and upon all occasions use and subscribe the name of Megan-Leanne Hendrick as my name in place of and in lieu of my former name of Megan-Leanne Redmond relinquished as aforesaid*

> 3. Expressly authorise and request all persons at all times hereafter to designate and address me by such assumed and adopted name of Megan-Leanne Hendrick only
>
> *In witness whereof I have hereunto subscribed my former name and adopted name this twenty-fifth day of January in the year of Our Lord eighteen hundred and thirty-four."*

All was in order, yet the tears welled once more in Megan's eyes as she second-read the scroll. It had all happened too quickly and yet the deed poll seemed to her the fitting and appropriate course to take. Some people are motivated by jealousy or fear, while with others it's pride or ambition. For Megan, propriety was everything. She must always do what conforms to social convention.

The next evening, Hendrick sat alone in his study. It being a Sunday the county office was closed. Yet in his determination he had resolved to call there at first light on Monday morning. Jacob, who had been installed as Robert Ferguson's successor on the latter's unceremonious discharge, could be trusted to hold the fort for a couple of hours.

Meantime Hendrick set about retrieving some vital documents that would accompany the deed poll to which Megan had acquiesced the evening before. The county office would expect him to present the child's Baptismal Certificate along with the original deed poll that his wife would have executed on her infant's behalf. He sifted through the lower drawers of his wife's desk until he happened upon that which he sought. It was a large envelope, dusty and with a somewhat tawny hue, that bore the following inscription in the unmistakable hand of his late wife:

"Statutory Documents Pertaining to Megan-Leanne"

He opened the envelope and peered inside. In the dim light afforded by his candle, he could descry that there were indeed two documents contained within. He withdrew the first and noted with some gladness that it was the Certificate of Baptism. All seemed in order. The document confirmed that *"one Megan-Leanne Hendrick, daughter to Mrs. Susanna Hendrick and Mr. Michael Hendrick, a turnip-snagger, was born at the noon hour on this third day of September in the year of Our Lord eighteen hundred and thirteen, in the village of Taghmon, in the barony of Shelmaliere West, in the County of Wexford."* This was perfect. All that he required now was the deed poll. But as soon he produced the second document and began to read it, he marvelled at his late wife's ingenuity. He sat smiling and, as he read the document aloud to himself, considered by how wide a margin he had underestimated that woman's resourcefulness. For it seemed that Susanna had, with unrivalled meticulousness, created a counterfeit of their daughter's Baptismal Certificate.

Highly unlawful as any such act was, Hendrick could not help but admire her for this masterstroke of creativity. The two documents were eerily similar. She had amended only that which it was necessary to amend; the surnames, the father's occupation, and the year of the birth. All other details were as per the original. Even the place of birth and the time of day were left unaltered. But what staggered the Mayor most of all was the painstaking effort his wife must have endured to copy the original handwriting so very precisely. It was flawless. Nothing had been left to chance in this superlative, albeit felonious, act of reproduction. The second document attested that *"one Megan-Leanne Redmond, daughter to Mrs. Susanna Redmond and Mr. Nicolas Redmond, a mariner, was born at the noon hour on this third day of September in the year of Our Lord eighteen hundred and fifteen, in the village of Taghmon, in the barony of Shelmaliere West, in the County of Wexford."* Leaning back in his chair, Hendrick set his mind to unravelling his wife's purpose. It rapidly became all too obvious to him. On whatsoever occasions it became necessary to evidence their daughter's birth for any official or statutory purpose, then the former—and legally correct—document could be produced. Yet should ever the innocent young girl request, out of mere curiosity, a glance at her own Baptismal Certificate, her mother would simply produce the latter, falsified, document. This was beyond genius as far as Hendrick was concerned. It was phenomenal. He even blessed his wife, poor woman, for her modesty in refraining from ever drawing his attention to such a masterpiece of forgery during her lifetime.

Furthermore, it solved another problem for him. If this was the course that his wife had chosen to take, then it seemed unlikely that she would have troubled herself with a deed poll after all. The girl was christened Megan-Leanne Hendrick and Hendrick was still her legal surname.

Clenching his fists this proud man punched the air with joy. He then produced from his pocket the deed poll he had coaxed the poor maiden into signing the previous night and cast the thing into the fire. He would of course visit Wexford Town the next day but only for Megan's sake and so he could keep up the pretence. She would, in her naivety, act as though her name was newly changed to Hendrick. Besides, he had already posted a notice to the offices of

The Castle & Bridge newspaper and any late withdrawal would have been both cumbersome and embarrassing. The Mayor had caused enough emotional upheaval for one weekend and well knew that it were best he proceed cautiously.

Megan-Leanne was still coming to terms with the previous night's revelation. If she expressed any doubts regarding her parentage he would simply produce the original Baptismal Certificate as irrefutable proof that she was beyond all doubt the daughter of one Mr. Michael Hendrick.

For now the Mayor would place the two documents back in their envelope and see that all was safely stowed. But as he held it open, he couldn't help but notice that in his fervour he had neglected to empty the envelope of its entire contents. There seemed to be another, far smaller, document contained therein. It was scarcely half the size of his own hand, if even that, and seemed to be a card or badge of some sort. He held the envelope upside down and keenly observed the small card as it slid out onto the desk. He recognised the design in an instant.

One of the tastefully prepared memorial cards procured by his wife upon the news of the sailor's drowning seemed to have found its way in amongst these documents relating to Megan. It was lying face down on the desk when he noticed that it differed slightly from those the two women had carried with them in the twelve months since they'd lost Redmond.

Yes, it was bordered with black. Yes, there was a large purple cross at the centre. But this time, curiously, that emblem of Christian faith was subscribed by the following two short lines of text:

> "Bless all the dear children
> In Thy tender care."

Where had he heard those words before? Of course he knew where he had heard them before. They were two lines of a well-known Christmas carol—one that was much loved, especially by Susanna. Two things, however, puzzled Hendrick just then.

Firstly, he wondered how a remembrance card relating to Nicky Redmond had found any place among documents collectively labelled as 'pertaining to Megan-Leanne'. Secondly—and perhaps even more disturbingly—he perceived how such a lyric, with its overt reference to the tender in years, sat uneasily on the memorial card of a sailor in his mid-forties. He placed his hand upon the card, sore afraid to turn it face up. He found that his glance had, almost subconsciously, been redirected to the two Baptismal Certificates still lying side by side on the desk.

Upon an instant his hand began to tremble. Hendrick felt like a man who may have stood before a great dam, a dam in which the sluices are severally opening before his very eyes and about which he is utterly powerless to avert the impending disaster. He had an intense foreboding that, should he turn the card and regard its full inscription, the dam would burst overwhelming his very soul with untold grief and anguish. His fears were well founded, for so it did. The Mayor took a deep breath, then turned the memorial card face up and read to himself, in horror, the following tribute:

> "In loving memory of Megan-Leanne Hendrick, age twenty months,
> who was taken from us, all too early, on the fourth day of May 1815,
> at Dungarvan, County Waterford. Gone but not forgotten."

A state of melancholy, which it was well nigh impossible to dispel, hovered over Hendrick. Though never in his life reputed as being particularly waggish by nature, the Mayor now wore an even more pronounced expression of lugubriousness than was his usual wont. Reclining in his chair, numb with grief, he ruminated on how harsh a blow fate had dealt him. He recalled in his mind his own extreme folly at Wellingtonbridge a near score of years before. Hendrick had often heard it stated that revenge is a dish best served cold. Yet never in his most daunting nightmares could he have anticipated what Susanna was contriving for his retribution during all that time.

His eyes were drawn towards a small desk calendar that stood on one of the upper shelves of the dresser. His erstwhile friend and confidant Robert Ferguson had, in an attempt to hold out an olive branch to the wretched Mayor, given it to him at Christmas as a gift. It was of a modest design, yet tastefully produced. But if there was one thing more than any other that characterised this calendar, it was that for each day of the year was printed a short excerpt from the Scriptures. On this particular day the verse held an especial poignancy for Michael Hendrick. It read:

> "Whoso diggeth a pit shall fall therein:
>   and he that rolleth a stone,
>   it will return upon him"

His glance returned to his daughter's memorial card, and then to the second of the Baptismal Certificates, the one that pertained to the living Megan-Leanne, the sailor's daughter. If this last article had been a legion of demons freshly despatched thence for his own torment, then he scarcely could have regarded it with more bitter distaste than he did just now.

As if the Mayor had not suffered jolting enough by these stark revelations, the door to his study was flung open in a flash. Before he could reprimand the maiden who had entered for consternating him in this fashion, that same young girl ran excitedly towards him. She flung her arms around the man with an affection that was almost as wild as to border on delirium.

"It's true, father, it's true. I know it's true. How could it be otherwise?" cried the girl, an unmistakable thrill in her voice. "I was all in a startle last night for I couldn't take it in all at once. But now I see the justice of it. It couldn't be any other way. I recalled every kind deed of yours and every kind word that you have bestowed on me since I arrived in Castlebridge. Yes father, right from the very moment I came into your office that afternoon and you gave me tea and cakes and all. And what about all the clothes that you've bought for me? It seems I only have to ask. There was that new dress in the spring, and the matching bonnet and gloves and shoes and all. I'll not mention the brand new mourning clothes you were very kind to dress me in when mother died. Those that I'd worn for the sailor would surely have done you know? There's scarcely a young maiden alive of such low birth upon whom so much is lavished. And I came to thinking to myself as I lay in bed 'what man would do all this for a mere *stepdaughter*?' No. From now on I'll call you my father and treat you like my father. I'll not call *him* that name at all. Any suitors I'm lucky enough to have will be brought before you father, as is fitting, for your approval. And someday, if that happy day ever comes, you'll be proud to give me away to him won't you?"

Hendrick pinioned the girl in his arms but said little. There was little to say. He had been so forthright with her in establishing his claim to paternity the night before that any recoiling from the stated position now would have been farcical in the extreme.

He smiled, but this was the expression of feigned affection. It was an arduous enough business for the Mayor to suffer the vengeance his wife had so guilefully planned to be thrust upon him from her grave. He had just learned of the death of his own daughter as an infant, of his own deception in believing the maiden in his household to be that daughter and of her true and now undeniable paternity. Yet now his penance was to become what pawnbrokers referred to as a mere 'united state security'. Hendrick owed his wife such a debt as could never be fully repaid. The longer he would lavish material gifts upon the girl whose paternity he had so doggedly claimed, the more conscious he would be that he was spending his own life on the daughter of a sailor whose very surname he had come to resent.

Megan-Leanne, wholly unenlightened in the matter as she was, hugged him one more time, kissed him, turned on her heels and went out of the room.

CHAPTER 10

❀

Too Close to Call

Renowned as they were for progress in all matters technological and agricultural, the inhabitants of Castlebridge were not folk to obstruct a popular tradition long observed. As each week commenced with a day reserved for rest and worship, so each would end with a day equally dedicated to fervent trading. Just as the morning of every First Day was heralded by a clanging of bells that summoned good folk all to church and chapel, so each Seventh would commence with the unmistakable tumult of market day. Though markets were also held on weekdays, it was on the Seventh Day that all the district's farmers, brewers, millers, cattle-dealers, corn-factors and hay-merchants et al bartered and transacted with stolid assiduity.

One particular Saturday in early March it was observed amid the clamour that, amongst the stalls baring the familiar and well-established names of "Hendrick", "Percival", "Breen", "Le Hunte", "Goodall", "Esmonde", "Nunn", "Shortle" etcetera, today was added the wholly unfamiliar "Ferguson". Of the Anglo-Norman families who'd landed at Wexford seven centuries earlier, few had settled beyond its boundaries. Consequently, their surnames gave them a strong Wexford identity and even outnumbered the county's indigenous surnames. The local traders were conscious of the remoteness of "Ferguson". Yet, with just one exception, they regarded the young man's venture as the mere even-handed trading of the world.

Not so with the irascible Hendrick. Noticing how freshly painted the trading sign was and how clearly the lettering stood out, he glared at it with intense detestation. If in lieu of his own surname the young man had traded under the title of "Outlander", "Blow in" or "Kingstown Upstart" then he would scarcely have been afforded any less society from the spiteful Mayor. The mere sight of Ferguson's stall, let alone the custom he'd been siphoning away Saturday by Saturday, galled Hendrick and only served to further intensify the steamed loathing he harboured for his rival. Ferguson, meanwhile, set out his stall that morning with all imaginable coolness.

The sorry episode with Amos Wickham had sowed the seeds of estrangement between the Mayor and Mr. Ferguson. Subsequently, that same enmity had firmly taken root at the market stalls. That it would be nurtured in more than one area of town life was inevitable.

Unlike the rural rotten boroughs where the local landlord was 'Sovereign', country towns were less undemocratic. In Castlebridge each Mayor was nominated by the sitting Corporation. He was then officially inaugurated at the Midsummer Fair in a ceremony traditionally presided over by the Chief Alderman. The mayoralty itself was set at two years, three being the maximum number of terms that any one Mayor could serve before being required to stand down. Thus it was, in the spring of eighteen thirty-four, that Mr. Michael Hendrick's sixth and final year as Mayor of Castlebridge drew to its close. It had widely been expected around the town that one Dr. Paddy Lambert, himself an alderman and much-respected member of the Corporation, would automatically succeed Hendrick to the post.

The Midsummer Fair was traditionally held on the fourth Saturday in June so the last date for nominations was set to the last Friday in March. Although the announcement of this date in the local newspaper was perceived as little more than a mere formality—it had been some fifty years since the position was last contested—doubts had started to be expressed in some circles about Dr. Lambert's fitness for the job. These were not a criticism of the man himself, for the doctor was a good and upstanding member of the community. It was however thought that he was too old, and it was also commonly known that he suffered from a litany of health problems which, although not life threatening for the present, showed few signs of abating. Lambert was a man of surpassing feebleness.

A significant number of councillors expressed unease at the notion of appointing anyone to this lofty position out of mere sentiment. One even prophesied that it may only be months before they would need to convene another such assembly to appoint his successor. It could be seen with half an eye that what was needed was a new broom and young blood to inject some fresh energy into the post.

"Beggin' yer pardon sir," said Alderman Roche placing one hand on Dr. Lambert's shoulder, "but I can't see the sense in puttin' that heart o' yours under any more pressure, least not for so little reward."

"Why don't we put it to him straight?" interjected Hendrick. "Do yeh want to be Mayor?"

"I surely do," replied the jovial Lambert.

"And are yeh really up to it?"

"I surely am."

"Well that settles it for me," concluded Hendrick.

It was not the end of the matter for the councillors however. On the very day that the nominations for Mayor would close a second name was added late to the ticket. And of all the names in Castlebridge it was the name of Mr. Robert Ferguson. As neither Dr. Lambert's pride nor his ambition permitted him to stand aside, this late development would automatically trigger a vote of the entire Corporation. Though the retiring Mayor could not ordinarily vote for his successor, Hendrick would unquestionably throw what weight he could behind the older candidate. He offered to manage Lambert's campaign and canvassed the other councillors aggressively.

Ferguson enjoyed popularity, but it was not universal. What some townsfolk admired as singleness of purpose, others perceived as stubbornness. A refined manner and Kingstown accent that some considered outward manifestations of an accomplished gentleman, others regarded as pompous and self-exalting pretence. One particular Sunday morning after church, when Ferguson had only lived in Castlebridge some four weeks, he overheard two local spinsters complimenting Reverend Whitley-Stokes on his sermon. As that week's topic was 'Prophets of The Old Testament', one of the ladies pertly remarked that Scripture was horribly male-dominated and what God's people wanted was a prophetess. Ferguson, presuming to interrupt this discourse, confidently named ten female prophets from memory. It was rumoured around the town, though not strictly true, that the merchant knew the entire Bible by heart. Wanting both humility and modesty, he was not everyone's first choice for Mayor.

The ballot date was set for a Thursday some three weeks hence and the respective campaigns seemed to be intensifying by the day. Hendrick's line was that the challenger was far too young, a mere thirty-one year-old. But his trump card was that the man had no experience whatsoever in local government, having only recently been co-opted to the Corporation.

The day of the ballot dawned and tension mounted in the Town Hall. Voting was scheduled to take place, in camera, between the hours of seven and eight. The result would then be announced a little after eight o'clock. By that time several of the locals had gathered outside and were milling around in eager anticipation of the result. Whatever outcome was to be announced little else would be discussed for many a night at The Pikeman's Inn or at any of the several other houses of refreshment in Castlebridge.

The eight o'clock bell had struck and several minutes had passed when Alderman Roche—a tall and lean man with large bristly eyebrows and a thin wiry chin—appeared holding a large sheet of paper and clumsily eying its details with his monocle. He raised his hands to the crowd and there was a general hush.

"As Chief Alderman of the Corporation," he began, straining his voice as if intending to be heard by the entire barony, "I do hereby declare that the total number of votes cast for each candidate at the election for Mayor held on this seventeenth day of April eighteen hundred and thirty-four is as follows. Lambert, Doctor Patrick, three votes. Ferguson, Mr. Robert, three votes. There were two abstentions."

When the din had subsided and the typical asides of 'a quare close thing' and 'a tied vote, would yeh credit that?' had all been exhausted, Alderman Roche continued.

"Given that the total number of votes cast for each candidate is equal and that no wan candidate can be deemed to have been elected, I hereby announce that a second ballot will be held two weeks hence, bein' the first day in May."

Engaging as town life in Castlebridge could oftentimes be, it was many a long year since the good folk of the neighbourhood had been treated to anything as electrifying as this. The Pikeman's Inn had been so thoroughly emptied for the announcement that Mr. Stafford himself stood at the door of that celebrated establishment trying as best he could to learn the result as it was declared. Had he failed in the task, however, he could not have been in ignorance for very long. Within minutes folk began to file back to the tavern and order their refreshments, doing so with an importunity that had poor Stafford scampering hastily back inside to brace himself and his good wife for the onslaught.

If the first campaign had been vigorous then the rematch would prove openly vindictive. Proud as they both were and with reputations to keep up, the candidates *themselves* remained on amicable terms. It was under the direction of Doctor Lambert's agent, the retiring Mayor, that rivalry descended into rancour and wrangle into overt combat.

Late on the evening of the first vote Hendrick had stood staring at his own reflection in the large mirror that hung over his opulently decorated mantelpiece. Not being a man of patience, even patience with himself, Hendrick kicked the lower tiles of his fire-hearth as he vowed to himself that 'such a rapscallion as Ferguson will not be Mayor o' Castlebridge as long as I'm alive'. The affronts that Hendrick had contrived for this young man and the slights he would attempt to put on his character over the next two weeks disturbed a little the conscience of the man he was so vigorously trying to get elected.

But Lambert admired something in Hendrick's spirit, energy and rugged earnestness, and did so in that curious way that folk always will admire qualities in others that they are in particular want of themselves. As April waned and the date for the second ballot drew near, there was scant evidence that any of the councillors who had voted in the first ballot had been cajoled into switching their preference.

The Chief Alderman had made no secret of his preference for Ferguson and it was generally perceived that Alderman Moses Cullen also admired the ambitious and energetic young Dubliner. The Doctor, meanwhile, had secured the loyal support of his two contemporaries Alderman Johnny Parle and retiring Deputy Mayor J. P. Nunn. There remained, however, the enigma of the two abstentions. Though not officially declared as such, it was tacitly understood that Tommy Cavanagh and Paddy Corish were the two men who had neglected to exercise their franchise on the first occasion.

Over those last two weeks of April both men were canvassed with an intensity scarcely to be believed. Had the numerous promises made to either been any more liberal then the successful candidate may well have opened himself up to a charge of bribery. Campaigning had reached such a pitch that the story of the election had found a place among the headlines of the county newspaper. But the Wexford World had chosen to concentrate wholly on the Mayor's jibing at Ferguson for the latter's not being a native of the county, etc. rather than on anything put out by the candidates themselves.

Whereas this was indifferent editorial, there was no denying that it was shrewd commerce. Sales of the newspaper soared to well nigh double that of the previous month. The notion that Castlebridge was on the verge of electing its first ever non-Wexford born Mayor had intrigued the entire county. Folks could be heard discussing the matter in many a public house, as far North as Camolin and Gorey, and as far West as Fethard and New Ross.

"Some young chap from up Dublin way I'm told, barely thirty year in the world," a crusty old man would say, pipe in one hand and tankard of stout in the other.

"Quare young isn't he?" another would add.

"Oh, aye," a third would offer, "the whole matter's quare as news from Bree if y'are askin' my opinion. All the same I'd have nottin' agin' him."

Campaigning over, the date finally arrived for the second ballot. If on the occasion of the first announcement there had been a small congregation, then it would be true to say that an entire throng seemed to have descended on the town for the second. Such a host had gathered that one could scarcely descry the local rustics of Simon Lowney and Christy Colfer amid the mob. Several of Hendrick's own workers had just strolled down from the mill having finished their duty at the hour of eight, among them the indomitable Nancy Muckridge and the infamous Amos Wickham. As once again Alderman Roche appeared on the town hall balcony the tension reached fever pitch. He stood there, declaration in hand, signalling to the crowd that he would not speak until the clamour had subsided. It inevitably did and Roche addressed his audience.

"As Chief Alderman of the Corporation," he began as before, "I do hereby declare that the total number of votes cast for each candidate at the election for Mayor held on this first day of May, eighteen hundred and thirty-four is as follows. Lambert, Doctor Patrick, four votes. Ferguson, Mr. Robert, four votes. There were no abstentions."

The whole affair could scarcely have been more suspenseful and reporters jostled with each other and with the townsfolk for any location that afforded a commanding view of the town hall's interior. The election of Hendrick's successor seemed an interminable process. All of the councillors as well as several other important officials were frantically running to and fro as a general sense of disarray, indeed one that bordered on hysteria, seemed to pervade the place.

Alderman Roche, as chief overseer on all such occasions, had had the foresight to enlist the help of Lawyer Creane and had endeavoured to send a horse and carriage to Wexford Town for that same professional earlier in the day. In the fading sunlight the two men could be observed in solemn conversation, the alderman nodding gravely as he absorbed all that the lawyer—an enormous man with several chins, each of which wagged profusely as he spoke—deliberated on such matters as 'precedents', 'prerogatives', 'casting votes' and such like. The current mayoralty had a mere eight weeks left to run and it was abundantly clear to all observers that the second ballot had resolved nothing. It had merely brought the town two weeks closer to inauguration day. Incertitude hung over the position like the sword of Damocles.

"It's merely a case," expounded the lawyer to the highly attentive Roche, "of distinguishing between a deadlock and an impasse. Here is an impasse. The precedent is such cases—"

"Alderman Roche," interrupted a gentleman. It was none other than Ferguson, "may I have a private word with you?"

Ferguson drew the anxious alderman into a small anteroom at the back of the town hall. This was noted by many but few conjectured on what its purpose might be. Seconds later Lawyer Creane's attention was distracted this time by Doctor Lambert, the latter evidently wishing to clarify the legal position pertaining to any such stalemates. Ceremonially affixing his spectacles, which hitherto had hung on a long black string suspended from around his colossal neck, Creane dusted off and opened one of the large leather-bound books of law he had taken with him to the count. Both men could be seen peering intensely at its contents. The doctor's expression evolved from one of distress to one of contentment and then even mild satisfaction. He looked around him in all directions as if scanning the entire length of the hall to seek out the attention of one person in particular.

If there was anyone in the neighbourhood of Castlebridge that night who was perceived as being serenely above all this frenzied pandemonium, then it was none other than the retiring Mayor himself—Mr. Michael Hendrick. As a storm of flummox pervaded the hall, Hendrick reclined pacifically in a corner and eyed all that was afoot. The Mayor was a learned man and knew full well what the next stage in process would be. *He* needed to consult no dusty law books. *He* needed no grossly overweight lawyer from Wexford Town to read him his rights. Furthermore it filled him with a warm sense of pleasure to know that nothing short of legal proceedings would obstruct the course that was imminently to be embarked upon.

For such was the precedent in elections for Mayor. Where there has been a requirement for a second ballot, and where that second ballot has proved inconclusive, then the retiring Mayor shall exercise a casting vote and the successful candidate shall forthwith be deemed to have been elected. Lambert moved celeritously down the hall towards where Hendrick was sitting. The gleeful expression on the doctor's face was telling enough. Hendrick raised his hand as if no words were required.

"I know it well, Lambert," he said to the doctor wearing a smug expression, "it's yours by default now. I only have to declare it to Roche and y'are home and dry."

Paddy Lambert shook the Mayor's hand gratefully. For Hendrick, the tied vote was just about the most desirable of all possible outcomes. Firstly, it had thrown the entire Corporation into a befuddlement entirely of their own making—a retiring Mayor does not traditionally nominate his successor and is barred from voting in any scheduled ballot—allowing Hendrick the spectacle of an eventful end to his tenure. Secondly, the new Mayor was unlikely to forget by how narrow a margin he had secured the post and Hendrick could reasonably expect an occasional favour from his successor. Thirdly, and rendering by far the most satisfaction to Hendrick, publicly exercising his casting vote in favour of Lambert was to be one last parting shot at Ferguson before his mayoralty ended. As this was something that Hendrick relished eagerly, he and Doctor Lambert began to search for Alderman Roche. They did not need to look far, for out of the anteroom emerged Roche accompanied by Robert Ferguson. Curiously, Ferguson then raised his hat to the other gentlemen, shook hands with Lambert, and went out of the building. As soon as he reached the outer gate he was assailed by a swarm of newspaper reporters, all of whom incessantly hurled a barrage of questions at him. But Ferguson answered to no single questioner.

"In view of tonight's inconclusive result," he began, "I have reconsidered my candidature and, deeming it to be in the best interests of Castlebridge, have officially informed Alderman Roche of my decision to withdraw from the contest. I have personally offered my congratulations to Mayor-elect Lambert and have also wished him every success in the honourable position to which he has been elected. I have no further comments at this stage other than a cordial invitation to my supporters to join me in rallying behind the doctor, and further to join me in a much needed drink at The Pikeman's Inn."

This last proposal was especially well received by the concourse. The gregarious assemblage of locals betook themselves to the bottom of the town and into the favoured tavern. There, they fortified themselves with ale. Ferguson soon joined them. But this last twist had been irksome to Hendrick. Yes, he had secured his friend's election at the expense of his bitter rival. But Ferguson had wrong-footed the Mayor late in the day, denying him that last pleasure he'd so fervently relished.

CHAPTER 11

A Grand Day Out

One Saturday a couple of weeks later, Hendrick ventured over dinner to engage his stepdaughter in conversation on a delicate matter.

"Megan," he said as they both tucked into their Wexford mutton, "do yeh know who I was talkin' to at the market this mornin'? Young Joey Fitzhenry."

"Joey Fitzhenry?" she enquired. "Whoever is he? I'm sure I've not heard tell of him."

"Of course y'aven't," answered Hendrick as if he'd expected the question. "He's not from 'round here. He's from three mile away, down by the sea at Curracloe."

At the mention of Curracloe Megan stopped chewing and her face reddened considerably. This change in the girl's countenance was not lost on Hendrick.

"I thought so. Now who was he? Out with it," demanded Hendrick in a tone of temperate remonstrance.

"Who?" she submitted, after a little hesitation. "I've no idea what you're on about father."

"Now there's no percentage in denyin' it. Joey Fitzhenry said he seen yeh a Sunda' or two ago, cusin' down the strand and yeh were engaged with someone. Fitzhenry didn't recognise the man but I just want to know his name. Is he respectable or will yeh be bringin' shame on this house, eh?"

"How could you say such things father?" she replied, clearly indignant at the suggestion. "It was only a friendly walk on a Sunday afternoon. Don't get fashed with me. You know how much I like to walk on Curracloe. Sure it's my favourite beach in the world. But don't speak rashly of a man when I haven't even told you his name. He's most respectable, wealthy too. I'm in love with him father and I hope someday he'll make me a fine husband even if you don't think so."

"Ah stop yer dreamin' and get on with it," cried Hendrick. "Who the devil is he?"

"His name," she said in answer to the coarsely blurted question, "is Robert Ferguson."

Hendrick gazed at the girl for a few moments and tried to imagine how cheated he could have felt were she really his flesh and blood daughter. But she wasn't. And he couldn't.

"Well just to let yeh know, Megan," he said, "that I'll not wish to interfere. If yeh love him then the business is fine by me. Just don't go bringin' any disgrace now, will yeh?"

Megan was stupefied. She would have preferred Hendrick's rebuke, even his open scorn, anything but this enigmatic indifference. It baffled the young maiden that the man who had showered her with such jealous paternal affection for so long now regarded her as merely another member of the household, a member with whom he just happened to share a surname. She further thought it bizarre that this transformation in his treatment of her had occurred at the end of January, the very time that he had so passionately declared himself to be her father. There was no evidence that Hendrick was in any way antipathetic towards her alliance with Ferguson. Megan-Leanne flinched slightly in disbelief and then continued her dinner. Some minutes later, the conversation resumed.

"Father," she said in kindly tones, "I know you'll be happy for me when you hear this news. Oh, it's nothing to do with Robert. Just some other news. I have been offered the chance of a position in a household. A wealthy lady, one of the wealthiest in the county I believe, is willing to take me on mainly as a servant but also for companionship. I'll have full board and a small allowance, ten shillings a week I think. What do you say father?"

"Sounds good to me. I'll not be stoppin' yeh."

Another look of pure astonishment on the face of the stepdaughter.

"But won't you miss me father?" she enquired.

"Of course, but yel surely be leavin' an address. I can write to yeh, can't I?"

"Oh, there's no need. The house is not far. It's Oldtown Manor."

"*Oldtown Manor?*" exclaimed Hendrick. "Mother o' Gad y'are movin' up in the world. It's only the richest folks can live at Oldtown Manor. Are the Nevilles still there? Is it them that's takin' y'on?"

"No. It seems the Nevilles have sold up. It's a lady from another part of the county. I don't know her name. But I start in July."

"Oldtown Manor?" Hendrick repeated. "There's no creditin' that. Well, good luck."

Some moments later Hendrick's maid arrived with the afternoon post. There was just one letter today and the Mayor noted with interest that it bore a Welsh postmark. If there had been one redeeming feature of the sorry business with Susanna's demise—complete with her revenge, administered post mortem, for his deserting her in their youth—it was that he was now free to marry the woman with whom he had been so indiscreet in Wales in his teens. It was indeed an ill wind that blew nobody any good. Hendrick could conceive of no reason in the world why he should not marry this woman, and there could be no question whether the letter he held in his hand was hers. He opened it and it read as follows:

Dearest Michael,

Having learned some two years ago that your wife had returned, and that you had chosen to settle with both her and your daughter, I readily dismissed those ambitions I'd harboured to move home to Wexford and marry you. Knowing Susanna to be alive, I should certainly not have thought of making any proposal to you upon any condition or understanding that you were necessarily to promise to unite yourself to me in the event of her demise. But I hoped that should any circumstance occur to effect her being dissevered from you indefinitely, you would allow me thereafter to consider myself at full liberty to embark upon any such course of action as I may at the time deem proper.

Last autumn news reached me that Susanna had passed away. I was truly sorry for your troubles, Michael, yet now I must hold you to your promise once more. I dearly wish to return to Wexford, to settle in Castlebridge, and to marry you. To return by Midsummer is my intent. You may well see me at the fair, which I understand is also the occasion for your standing down.

Sometime this summer, perhaps the better side of Susanna's anniversary, I would plead with you to meet me. We can allow the townsfolk to perceive us as strangers, then meet, then court, and then marry. Occasions for spending time together will be more frequent than perhaps you had expected. I trust your daughter has informed you of her offer. Yes, Michael, it is I who has bought Oldtown Manor. I look forward to your first visit. May the day be not too long delayed.

Yours always,

Miss Lucy Devereux.

At last, Michael Hendrick had a cause for rejoicing. His first wife was gone almost a year, the duties of Mayor, which had of late become burdensome to him, would soon be lifted from his shoulders and finally Lucy Devereux was to move to Castlebridge, to live in Oldtown Manor, and marry him.

As May drew to its close and the month of June ushered in the long, sultry, dog days of summer, preparations were well underway for the winding down of Hendrick's six-year mayoralty. Yet with every bit as much consideration so were those for Lambert's inauguration and all the festivities that would accompany it. It was a local tradition, come the Midsummer Fair, to cease trading in the town's market at noon as this would facilitate any finishing touches required to the day's planned diversions. This year was no exception. And so it was that Saturday the twenty-eighth of June dawned, doing so bright and fair as could be wished for.

By two o' clock Castlebridge was primed for a thoroughly enthralling afternoon and stalls were erected at every conceivable location. The activities were multifarious. Several of the town's children amused themselves at the countless game stands, while those with keen eyes for a bargain seized on the once-yearly opportunity to purchase five of the tastiest 'farthing-toffees' for just one penny. Others were held captive by the prestidigitations of a visiting conjurer. Others still sat patiently but excitedly before a face-painter so that some twenty minutes later their faces were all in a glow—purple on the right cheek, yellow on the left. As those same children, eager as they were to identify with the ancient tribes of their county, keenly observed the parade pass on the street, the sight of their countenances so illumined was certain to have a dazzling effect on any visitor to the county. Yet even those folk of more mature years, or children whose parents considered their own progenies serenely above all such contrivances, could not wholly avoid involuntarily sporting the county colours, as inadequately suspended bunting gently drooped and flapped against their faces in the calm summer breeze.

Many of the town's prominent business folk also graced the event with their presence. There was Mr. Bulger the wine merchant, Tommy Bent the horse dealer, Kehoe the pig breeder and Colloton the auctioneer. These were soon joined by Leary the baker and, a little later, Jordan the butcher—both of whose businesses were located at the bottom of the town near to the canal bridge. Then there were the familiar faces of Simon Lowney and Christy Colfer who, together with their comrade Nancy Muckridge, positioned themselves at Main Street's half-way point, just where Gorey Road sloped down to meet it from the northeast of the town. This strategic location afforded as commanding a view of the famed exposition as could be contrived.

The Midsummer Fair, always the liveliest and best attended of the town's four annual fairs, assumed an even greater momentousness when coupled with the swearing-in of a new Mayor. It was no time for half measures. Of all the town's customs that folk so vehemently defended and so faithfully observed, folk indeed quite content to live in blissful ignorance of the origins of those same traditions, the inauguration of a new Mayor was arguably among the most eccentric. Yet to depart from any one of the town's famed and long-standing formalities would have been to perpetrate an unspeakable abomination upon the good folk of the town. 'It was good enough for them as went before us and it's surely good enough for us' was the standard retort, both among the townsfolk of Castlebridge itself and genial rustics of the county 'round.

As precedent had dictated, the inauguration of the town's new Mayor proceeded thus. At the top of the town, where Main Street veered onto Codd's Walk, stood both the Chief Alderman and the retiring Mayor. The incumbent positioned himself so as to face downhill while the Chief Alderman, facing in the opposite direction, fixed his frame directly in front of the Mayor with his own back to the town. The Chief Alderman produced a long rectangular wooden box, bordered with steel, and opened it ceremoniously. In an act of staged humility he then bowed low to the Mayor. The chain of office was removed and placed meticulously into the box. Carrying the box in one hand and its lid in the other, the Chief Alderman then walked backwards, in as formal a stride as he could feign, the entire length of Main Street with his gaze all the while fixed on the retiring Mayor.

This most ludicrous of rites was rendered even more comical by its necessitating that same Alderman to clothe himself in a most preposterously voluminous red gown for the purpose. Indeed so precarious did Roche's position seem just then that many of the younger townsfolk ventured to wager on whether he might not trip up, speculating on the untold hilarity among onlookers were a sight so farcical ever beheld. But Roche, dependable as ever, maintained his poise. He was a man well reputed to execute the duties of his office with no little dignity. Officiating thus, he crossed the canal bridge and greeted the gaunt and cadaverous figure of Doctor Lambert.

"Hear now ye townsfolk of Castlebridge and all folk of goodwill," roared Alderman Roche at the crowd before then turning to the doctor. "Do you, Doctor Patrick Lambert of Ardcavan Road, Castlebridge, accept the title Mayor of Castlebridge? Will you perform, with the help of Almighty God, the duties of this office to the utmost of your abilities? And will you exercise your authority as best serves the interests of the town?"

"I surely will," came the emphatic reply, Lambert beaming from ear to ear.

Next came the precise moment for Alderman Roche to offer the chain of office to the doctor, which the latter duly removed from its wooden box and placed over his own neck. At this, Alderman Roche covered the box once more, placed it on the ground before him and, lifting a hand to either side of his mouth as a natural aid to vocal amplification, bellowed the following proclamation.

"Know ye all that are present here today, that your town this day hath taken unto itself a new Mayor, and that he be one Doctor Patrick Lambert of Ardcavan Road. Hark! If anyone saith that he be not Mayor, or denieth the authority vested in him, then let whosoever be counted among the accursèd of the barony. Oh yea, oh yea, oh yea!"

This flamboyant exclamation was followed by a short prayer, which in turn was succeeded by Roche taking up his wooden box and, accompanied by the new Mayor at his side, parading back up Main Street to the erect figure of the outgoing Mayor. The new Mayor then cordially shook hands with his predecessor—a solemnity for which protocol had dictated, for some bizarre and long-forgotten purpose, that the left hand should be utilised—and then followed this freakish ritual with a speech that was unostentatious, if not self-abnegating.

Though Lambert was not reputed as having a particularly loquacious disposition, this final act in the afternoon's drama was generally perceived as being a good deal more protracted than the occasion warranted. For those who had not gathered in close proximity to the Mayor the tedium was exacerbated by Lambert's low-pitched and languid voice. Today's peroration agitated many. After several minutes Christy Colfer and Nancy Muckridge could be overheard mocking their new Mayor. They particularly drew attention to how such qualities as forwardness and self-assuredness were so conspicuously wanting in the man. These animadverts were at such a distance as to be inaudible to the Mayor himself, while not lost on many of the rustics gathered round.

"He should be takin' a leaf out o' the clergymen's book, he should," opined Colfer banteringly. "Them folks are learned how to talk distinctly so we can hear them good 'n' clear."

"They surely are!" concurred the unpolished Muckridge. Then turning to Colfer, Simon Lowney and assorted other locals, she raised three fingers and, to the gratifying amusement of her peers, exhorted the commonly held sentiment that all orators do their hearers no small service when they "*Stand* up, *speak* up and *shut* up!"

Despite the popularity that this noble and honourable doctor had long enjoyed in the neighbourhood, there was in many quarters great unease regarding his appointment as Mayor. Even on his own inauguration day, attired for the purpose as elegantly as any gentleman would be expected to, Lambert could scarcely hide his own frailty. The man's unassertive nature, the timidity in his failing voice and the sight of his crumpled, feeble frame, all conspired to arouse the solicitude of the townsfolk that his would likely be a rather anaemic mayoralty. Be that as it may, it *had* been settled that he was Mayor, and the Corporation had pledged him its unconditional support for as long as he should remain in the post.

CHAPTER 12

❦

The Choices of Lucy Devereux

On the day immediately following the Midsummer festivities Hendrick sat pensively in his study, soberly considering all that his future might have in store. The previous day's ceremonies had all been acted out as tradition dictated. Yet the retiring Mayor was all the while moderately concerned by one aspect of the business, namely the conspicuous absence of one Miss Lucy Devereux. Referring once again to the correspondence he had received from her some weeks earlier, he was served a reminder of how non-committal the woman had been in relation to the precise date of her arrival in Castlebridge, how to arrive by Midsummer was her 'intent', and how he 'may well' see her at the fair. He shrugged his shoulders resignedly, folded the letter and replaced it in its envelope.

But his fears were ill founded, and owed rather more to an impatient disposition on *his* part than to any laxity or negligent unpunctuality on *hers*. For it came to pass that the very next Saturday, being the first Saturday in July, local carpenter Pierce Kyan observed an opulently decorated chaise driving towards Castlebridge from the direction of Wexford Town. As it trundled northward along Ardcavan Road it came to an abrupt halt on the southern outskirts of the town, some three hundred or so yards short of The Pikeman's Inn. The driver could then be descried turning to his passenger to courteously make some enquiry of the same. The passenger was a tall and lavishly dressed woman of about forty. She wore a crimson dress that was both extensive and elegant, yet classy and not lurid. Consistent with the fashion of the day the dress was designed to fit tightly above the waist. This had the effect of lending its wearer a proud posture. But in the case of this woman, it also served to highlight the flexuosity of her slim and shapely figure. She also donned stylishly long white gloves and a drawn cotton bonnet.

This passenger gracefully waved a hand in the direction of the adjoining road, in consequence of which the driver then doffed his bowler hat to her, nodded and then directed the horse and carriage in a sharp right-hand turn. They proceeded along the road leading to a south-eastern precinct known as Ardcolm. Some half a mile or so along the road the entourage halted again, this time outside a tasteful and elegant estate. It was comprised of a large and fashionable mansion on spacious and well tended grounds. The name of the property was Oldtown Manor. The driver promptly dismounted then dutifully and deferentially stood beside the chaise offering a ready hand to the passenger. She alighted from that conveyance with ease.

"Oldtown Manor, Miss Devereux," said the man in submissive tones, bowing once more. He was both her driver and her butler.

"That'll do Hartley," said the lady addressing him in an assertive yet inoffensive tone as she surveyed her new residence with an obvious expression of satiety. "Very Good."

The grandeur and exclusivity of Oldtown Manor were rivalled only by the abounding wealth and affluence enjoyed by those who could ever have afforded to reside in the place. Its own hallway was palatial, its chambers exquisite, its dining and leisure rooms luxurious in the extreme. In terms of wealth and renown, Oldtown Manor was to Ardcolm what Ardcolm was to Castlebridge, while Ardcolm was to Castlebridge what Castlebridge was to the county. The very place itself boasted an overt plenitude about which most of the county's population could only fantasise. But Lucy Devereux was indeed a woman of means, being herself no stranger to stylishly fashionable domiciles on vastly spacious tracts of land.

"I must inform you Hartley," remarked the lady, the latter carrying her luggage towards the manor's lavish porch, "that you will soon be joined, I should hope this very weekend, by a young lady who is to enter my service and also live at the manor as my companion."

"Very well, ma'am," the servant replied respectfully as he stood in the hall, cases in hand and awaiting further instructions.

Lucy Devereux then instructed Hartley as to precisely where he was to place the various items she had brought with her to the manor. Two more carriages had left Wexford Town that very afternoon and would arrive within the hour.

As the butler stood patiently on Oldtown Manor's large gravelled drive he noticed not two, but rather three, carriages busily wheeling their way up the Ardcolm Road and doing so as if in procession. All three carriages turned into the grounds, passed through the gateway and rattled along in the general direction of the self-possessed butler. The first and second of the carriages were laden with the remainder of Miss Devereux's possessions. This was as the butler had expected. But the third carriage, though burdened with similarly copious quantities of possessions as either of the others, also carried on it a good-looking young girl of barely twenty winters, if that. Hartley deduced that this must be the young maiden Miss Devereux had spoken of, who was to join the lady's service as well as to relieve her solitude.

"This *is* Oldtown Manor, is it not?" enquired the girl interestedly. "Does a Miss Devereux reside in this place by chance?"

"She surely does," returned Hartley offering the same courtesies upon the girl's alighting from her carriage as had been afforded to Lucy Devereux some hour or so earlier. "Mistress is expecting you. I will go and see if she is disposed to receive you now. Eh, may we have the pleasure—"

"Megan," interposed the girl earnestly. "Tell her that Megan-Leanne Hendrick has arrived and awaits her pleasure."

Hartley bowed once more and, seconds later, re-emerged to invite the young girl into the house.

"Miss Devereux is in the drawing room," the butler confirmed. "Mistress has been suffering from a little indigestion today but she eagerly wishes to see you."

From the hour that Megan-Leanne set foot inside the sumptuously chic interior of Oldtown Manor and was cordially introduced to its truly genteel proprietress, it was instantly obvious to both women that their companionship was destined to be verifiably symbiotic in every sense of that word. For Megan's part, she had departed from under the roof of a truly enigmatic man. He had passionately pleaded with her to treat him as the father he had claimed to be only to reciprocate that unassuming loyalty with a cold and unfeeling nonchalance towards her. In fact, he had done so almost from the moment of his own zealous appeals for her daughterly devotion. Now she was to be employed and cared for, indeed cherished, by this exceptionally genteel and cultivated woman of means. Her new domesticities were far more to her liking than had been those from which she had recently departed.

If Megan had wanted for *little* at Slaneyview House, then she would want for *nothing* once ensconced at Oldtown Manor. Now holding down a position originally advertised as 'servant and companion', Megan would soon discover to her lasting satisfaction that it entailed far more of companionship than of servility. Furthermore, the woman was some twenty years her senior and seemed likely to fill something of the role of mentor to her. Indeed, the thought had already taken root in Megan's chaste and innocuous mind that soon she might seek the counsel of her new friend on matters amorous. 'I wonder what she'd make of Robert' the maiden would muse to herself sitting in front of the large decorative mirror in her spacious, high-ceilinged bedroom. 'I'm only the daughter of a merchant myself so she can hardly say he's beneath my station, even if she wishes me to marry a gentlemen who is in some measure more accomplished.'

The innocent girl even conjectured on how her new mistress—limitlessly generous as the woman appeared to be—might assist her were the liaison with Robert to take its natural and honourable course. A portion of the seemingly inexhaustible wealth at Miss Devereux's disposal would surely be made available should Megan and Robert ever unveil plans of a matrimonial nature. At any rate, the rapport she enjoyed with her mistress was certain to be a great source of personal enrichment for the girl in and of itself. But if this most convenient of alliances could be deemed to be reasonably beneficial to the younger woman, then there could be no denying that it was to be most emphatically expedient to Miss Devereux.

"What a most excellent 'esprit de corps' there exists between us dear," offered Miss Devereux to her young friend as they both sat sipping coffee in the spacious garden of their new and magnificent abode. Megan wondered whether such phrases were popular among women of society. She was however no stranger to the French language, having lived in Quebec for three years. Lucy Devereux threw back her head and held a piece of lightly buttered croissant in the air. "Don't mind my little eccentricities. I'm sure I can't help it, you know. These French phrases just escape my lips sometimes. It runs in the family if you like. I must tell you something of the history of my family. Wouldn't you rather like to hear that?"

Megan nodded her consent. Lucy Devereux then proceeded to expatiate on the rather intriguing history of her illustrious family; how the Devereux name had originated in a town in France called Evreux, how her mother's name "de la Roche" had also been connected with that country as well as with Wales where Lucy had herself lived for many years, how the town of her own birth,

Adamstown, was so named in honour of her ancestor Adam Devereux, and how she herself fluently spoke three languages—alternating between English, French and Welsh as circumstances dictated. There seemed no limit to this woman's linguistic capacity. She even had an adequate command of Latin and Irish, as well as of a strange language named Yola that Megan had never heard of before.

As has already been remarked, this polished and educated lady had contrived the means of re-uniting with Michael Hendrick by a most ingenious, yet simple and foolproof, arrangement. Later that very morning, Hartley came into the drawing room holding a tray on which there was a letter addressed to one 'Miss Lucy Devereux'. He handed it to the lady of the house and left the room forthwith. The contents of the letter were as follows.

Dear Lucy,

I'm reliably informed that you are now settled in at Oldtown Manor. I had expected to see you at the fair in June. Perhaps you'd got yourself waylaid. These last few days I'd almost given up on you returning at all to be honest. But the matter is better late than never.

As you have so cleverly suggested, I will make it my business to call regularly to Oldtown Manor during the summer, doing so as if to visit Megan. Best to let things lie for a few weeks yet don't you think? Perhaps early August I'll make a first visit. Megan can introduce us and then we can court soon after as planned, assuming one living in such manorial splendour can lower herself so much as to be seen in company with an ordinary middle-class barley-dealer like myself.

Yours,

Mr. Michael Hendrick
Slaneyview House
Codd's Walk.

Lucy Devereux sighed audibly upon discerning the sentiments expressed by this quick-tempered man. Firstly it was *she* who had so ardently and unremittingly sought *his* commitment to marry. Secondly it was *she* who had undergone the upheaval of returning to Wexford and setting up home in a town with which she was not over-familiar. Thirdly it was *she* who had devised the rather ingenious plan for their re-unification, a plan which would have the welcome side-effect of furnishing *his* daughter (or so both women believed her to be) with employment and a secure home.

Furthermore she resented her former lover's insinuation that she may consider herself socially above a man of his station. For Lucy Devereux was unparalleled with regard to the benevolent recognition that she invariably displayed for the middle classes—a respect that was, sadly, all too conspicuous by its absence among much of the landed gentry in that particular era. *They* seemed helplessly predisposed to consider any person beneath them as belonging to a different species. *She* regarded middle-class folks almost as honorary members of polite society but who, either by some misfortune or by providential chance—she was not to know—were required to engage in the most inconvenient business of gainful employment for their survival and betterment in all matters pecuniary.

The woman was indignant at the tone of her former lover's correspondence and, in her annoyance, determined there and then to reply to this most impertinent of epistles. Thus another letter was worded, signed, sealed and handed to Hartley to dispatch with all manner of haste. Lucy's reply ran thus:

Dear Michael,

Thank you for a most engaging letter. My late arrival in Castlebridge was unavoidable. My boat had arrived on the Friday, the day immediately prior to the fair, yet I had left a good deal of unfinished business upon setting out from Wales. I determined therefore to spend some week or so at Wexford Town. I took out accommodation at Aspel's Hotel until such time as the transfer of ownership of Oldtown Manor had been legally accomplished. There were documents to be signed and sealed. The whole business was really most bothersome. I make no apology for my tardiness however. You, Michael, kept me waiting for twenty-four years!

I do fervently anticipate your first visit here. Early August would indeed be opportune. So far as I can recall, Sunday the third is Susanna's anniversary and I therefore assume you will require a degree of privacy with your daughter on that particular day. Perhaps you have arranged to meet together at the cemetery but the entire business is a matter for you both. Might I be permitted to comment, in passing, that Megan is a delightful young lady and is most undeniably a credit to you.

My residence is at Ardcolm, yours at Codd's Bridge. Our respective dwellings' being located at diametrically opposite ends of the town will most assuredly lessen the likelihood of any embarrassing and irksome encounters between us in the days prior to your first calling at the Manor.

Michael, I rather take exception to your intimation that I harbour suspicions regarding the suitability of the professional classes where marriage is concerned. You know full well how I enjoy a reputation as something of a sui generis in this regard.

Furthermore, as it is difficult not to be sensible that there are many special circumstances in our situation that render it of the utmost importance that our secret remains ours alone, you'll be aware that any disclosure of our earlier correspondence, whether to the general public or alone to your daughter, would be to the detriment of both our reputations. Such revelations would irreparably damage my good name and be highly injurious to yours.

I renew my trust in your continued discretion.

Yours always,

Miss Lucy Devereux
Oldtown Manor
Ardcolm.

It was with a combined expression of anticipation and discomposure that Lucy Devereux stood restively by the large and heavy-curtained back window of her spacious drawing room during the late afternoon of that first Saturday in August. She had conjectured that her former lover might call to the manor that very day after market, being the afternoon immediately prior to his late wife's first anniversary. This would afford Hendrick the perfect excuse for a visit, acting all the while as though the sole purpose of his calling was to discuss with Megan-Leanne the details of any commemorative arrangements set in place for the following afternoon.

Megan-Leanne herself was in fact absent from the estate just then, and Lucy fancied rather that her young companion was out on some errand or most likely keeping company with the young barley-merchant the maiden had been speaking of so admiringly in recent days. A visit from Hendrick would now be timely indeed, as it would afford to both parties the confidentiality required for the discussion of sensitive matters. It happened that just as these considerations were revolving in the mind of Lucy Devereux, there came a loud knock on the front door of the manor. Hartley was immediately sent for.

"I've been expecting this visitor for some time, Hartley," she said with delicate finesse. "Tell the gentleman that I await his pleasure in the drawing room. Then send him thither."

"Yes Miss Devereux."

Lucy then composed herself for the impending encounter and stood near the drawing room's rear window in an attitude of feigned placidity. She was nervous and could scarcely hide her trepidation. As the sound of the visitor's footsteps fell on her ears, growing louder as he approached, the woman's agitation increased almost by the second. Yet she determined to receive Mr. Hendrick courteously and resolved to be civil in all respects.

When Megan finally did return from her afternoon's adventures, Lucy would simply tell her friend that she had bidden the man to forestall his departure pending his daughter's imminent return and had politely invited him to partake of some afternoon tea and hot scones. This could readily be perceived as the first ever encounter between the two and Megan-Leanne, naïve as she was, would have no grounds for suspicion were their relationship to blossom and flourish. The drawing room door slowly opened and this was accompanied by a gentle knock that was barely audible. Taking one deep breath Lucy Devereux turned about and confronted her visitor, doing so with a confident and self-assertive expression on her face.

But her scheme was derailed in an instant. It simply did not occur to the lady that her visitor might be any person other than the former Mayor. But the aspect of this unexpected visit that had scuppered her plans so thoroughly lay not in the fact of her visitor's being someone other than Michael Hendrick. No, for the man who stood before her was not 'good-looking', 'polished' or 'agreeable'. He was the most handsome creature she had seen in all her days.

That very moment was a turning point in Lucy Devereux's life. It would require her to completely redefine to herself what profound unthinking physical attraction actually entailed. From that day, that very instant indeed, food would never taste the same, scenery never look the same, music never sound the same. From the second of August eighteen thirty-four, Lucy Devereux would never have to *imagine* true, unreasoning infatuation. She had *encountered* it. Or rather it had been thrust upon her, leaving her veritably smitten by its spontaneous allure. If ever a lady was capable of being captivated by a man's unforced charm it was then.

The gentleman was tall and of average build, some six or seven years her junior, and carried about with him a magnetism that was all but mesmerising to her. She stood motionless, captivated by his deep-set, sparkly blue eyes and his youthful visage. He had short, reddish-blonde hair as well as curly sideburns that complemented his long, clearly defined jawbone. He was neatly dressed, his expression was pleasing and his manner kindly. In fact, Lucy Devereux perceived his mere presence to be an enchantment in itself. Showing some small degree of deference to the lady by removing his bowler hat he began to speak to her in a distinctly unfamiliar, yet in her view not unpolished, accent.

"Eh, it's possible I've called at the wrong time. I do beg your pardon, Mrs. eh—"

"Devereux," she interrupted, her eyes fixed upon his. "My name is *Miss* Lucy Devereux," she added with particular emphasis on the title. Then offering her hand to him she declared how she was pleased to make his acquaintance. This was most probably the understatement of the century. His tender act of humility in taking her free hand and kissing it all but sent the woman into ecstasy. Her eyes wore an intensely glazed expression as she continued to stare at him and the two spoke no words for some moments. Nervously changed his hat from one hand to the other and then back again, her visitor now shiftily broke the silence.

"Eh, I had hoped," he continued, with reserved composure, "that Miss Hendrick would be at home today. It was her I had intended to call upon. Oh, and I must beg your pardon once again. I never told you my name. It's Ferguson. My name is Robert Ferguson. I'm a barley-merchant in the town you know, though I'm not from these parts originally. I come from the Port of Kingstown near Dublin. I'm certain you've heard of it."

"Many times," remarked Lucy, her glance still intently fixed upon the treasure she so jealously craved. "My people hail from some leagues away in Adamstown, though I have lived much of my life in Wales. And don't think that your accent sounds any way outlandish in *my* ears. In fact I think it's rather charming, and so I shall grant you what you have asked for."

"Pardon me Miss Devereux but I don't believe I've *asked* for anything," Ferguson replied hesitantly and wearing an expression of mildly amused perplexity.

"Oh yes you have, three times now, my *pardon*. And I give it to you."

"Charming," replied Ferguson raising his eyebrows, another protracted period of silence following the remark.

Lucy's unfettered preoccupation with this young man may be supposed to have been benign enough with regard to any effect it seemed likely to have on the merchant's existing associations with Megan-Leanne—sweethearts as they had been for some three months now—were it not for the indisputable fact that, whether Lucy sensed it at first or not, the feeling was comprehensively reciprocated on the part of Ferguson. His first glance at this incredibly classy woman had impassioned the man in a manner that left poor Megan-Leanne in the halfpenny-place. Yes Megan-Leanne was pretty, but this woman was ravishing. Megan-Leanne may have had cute dimples and a gleaming smile, but a tangible aura of desirability hung all around Lucy Devereux. The lady's dark, wavy hair, her seductively large brown eyes, her soft, sallow skin—not to mention a figure that epitomised perfection in feminine shapeliness—all conspired to hold the young man in a daze.

In spite of the concord among all the worthy bachelors of Castlebridge that Megan had the finest looks in the barony, it was also tacitly understood, if not sometimes candidly admitted, that the maiden had little else to recommend her. The girl was neither shy nor forthright, neither jocular nor grave, and was as far removed from the two extremes of intellectual brilliance and unlettered nescience as it was ever possible to imagine being. Even before his wholly unexpected encounter with Miss Devereux, Robert Ferguson had grasped the cold realisation that, apart from her undeniable handsomeness, there was at this time no one characteristic that defined this much admired girl more than any other. She was at that time, in every matter other than physical form, a very ordinary companion to him.

Lucy Devereux, on the other hand, held a fascination for him that he had never believed possible. The woman radiated an ethereal beauty and a high-toned, elegant, charm that were well nigh bewitching to him. Megan was agreeable. But he would apotheosize this woman. His own jitteriness in their initial encounter was, thus, wholly accounted for, as Robert Ferguson was enraptured by the mere proximity of this sumptuous, cultivated and artistic woman. The slight disparity in their respective years, of which an issue might otherwise have been made, paled into insignificance now. She invited the barley-dealer to be seated and beckoned to Hartley to fetch the afternoon tea that had been in readiness for the arrival of Michael Hendrick.

The unseen barriers that had been so artificially contrived for preserving a clear segregation between members of the three distinct social classes were on no account peculiar to Castlebridge, or even to Wexford. Ferguson well knew, hailing as he did from an environment where the repulsive and hideous face of that same dehumanising social cancer was evidenced daily in all its malignancy and depraved nefariousness, that the woman for whom he already harboured matrimonial ambitions may consider him below her station. Yet in comparative terms at least, the companionship of the professional classes was enjoyed, or at the very least tolerated, by the landed gentry with a good deal more magnanimity than was the companionship of common labourers by either.

The time was, after all, during the reign of the unassuming King William the Fourth when parliamentary reform was the order of the day. The county franchise had not been updated for four centuries, leaving the Kingdom with a dilapidated and ineffective system of representation that only benefited the aristocracy. The House of Lords had recently been cajoled into passing The Reform Act of 1832, browbeaten into doing so under a threat from William that he would create enough new peerages to secure its passage should they fail in the task. Thus, the voting franchise was extended beyond county freeholders and was for the first time ever afforded to all middle class landowners.

Much of the landed gentry perceived such legislation as a snowflake that heralded a blizzard. And well they might, for The Reform Act would form the basis for further acts to eventually enfranchise all adult subjects. The fight for democracy was sweeping Europe, with dire consequences for royalty. In Britain and Ireland the camel's back was beginning to bend and creak. The aristocracy was, by stealth, being relieved of its several privileges. Ferguson offered his bowler hat to the servant and then lowered himself into a large comfortable chair to regard this fascinating woman further.

"I had not imagined," began his host, "that Megan could have been quite so fortunate in her suitors, notwithstanding her local reputation as something of a 'femme fatale'."

Ferguson blushed, then stirred uneasily but made no reply. Lucy Devereux sat herself down in the chair opposite and Hartley returned with the refreshments. When he had exited, Miss Devereux engaged her visitor in conversation once more, this time inserting those phrases of a truly Gallic origin with rather more deliberation than she had done during her exchanges with Megan-Leanne. This had a dazzling effect on her visitor.

"It would appear that young Miss Hendrick is out on an errand of some kind. But you must visit again. Your company is most agreeable and you pronounce my family name just as our French cousins do. It's so charming, so, I don't know, polished or something. The Wexford folk call us '*Dev*-ricks'. You are rather 'à la mode' for your station, are you not? I, at any rate, find your society rather intriguing." If Lucy Devereux had at that moment been honest with herself, she might have been tempted to substitute 'sensuously seductive' for 'rather intriguing'. "Why don't you attend Sunday lunch with us tomorrow? That would be most delightful. It's Boeuf à la Meunière this week I believe. We dine at two on Sundays."

"Two o'clock?" repeated Ferguson. "Isn't tomorrow Mrs. Hendrick's anniversary? Won't young Megan be with her father at the graveside?"

Lucy reclined languorously, then raised her eyebrows and lowered them again—all without releasing the merchant from her glance. Ferguson perceived her intentions in an instant and, after a degree of internal deliberation, nervously but cordially accepted her invitation to dine.

CHAPTER 13

❁

Rash Dealings

The following Saturday Megan-Leanne sat alone in her chambers. In her profound reverie the maiden was blissfully ignorant of the recent turn of events that was to cause so much upheaval. Lucy Devereux, two storeys below in the drawing room, was however engaged in a most frightful of confrontations.

"What in the name o' God are yeh playin' at, woman?" cried a ferocious voice. "Yeh write to me for years, beggin' me t'ave yeh, then y'up shop and move to Castlebridge for my sake. Don't be denyin' that yeh came to Castlebridge for that wan purpose. I bide me time for a few weeks as yeh tell me, now I turn up and y'are all cold to me and sayin' there's an end to it. Well beshrew me if I've seen nottin' as brazen in all me days."

"I'll not be spoken to in such an insolent manner, Michael," remonstrated Lucy in all the singular contrariority of her self-possession, "not by you nor by anybody else. And don't use phrases like 'beshrew me' in polite company. Such utterances are really most uncouth. I am a lady. Don't you folks have any idea how to speak to a lady?"

"I'll give yeh speakin' to a lady alright if it's givin' me the run-around y'are at, woman," cried Hendrick deprecatingly. The man was visibly fuming at this most recent twist of fate. He composed himself a little as if seeing the futility of his ire. Then he continued. "I'll give yeh a little time, Lucy, to change yer course. I'll come back to yeh at th'end o' harvest and learn yer mind. I have somethin' on yeh Lucy and yed better be treadin' carefully. I'll give yeh 'til Halloween to consider it. It's me that should be yer rightful husband and yeh can't be gainsayin' it."

"There is one favour, Michael, that I would ask of you," added the lady seemingly unnerved by Hendrick's implicit threat. Lucy Devereux had a modicum of stoicism that enabled her to remain calm and composed even under intense pressure. She now appealed to her former lover in less confrontational tones. "Like a gentleman," she continued imploringly, "you will do me the favour of returning to me all the letters I sent you during the last twenty-four years will you not?"

Hendrick stared at the woman fixedly and could read the unease that was written across her visage just then. Wishing to bring no calumnies upon himself however, he had already quite made up his mind in this regard and had resolved to remain discreet in every respect. He had determined to conceal the various epistles from general view. Yet it seemed gratifying to the man to procrastinate in returning them to their originator, as if her fretting on the issue would seem proper justice for the manner in which she had so abruptly banished him from her plans.

"I suppose," he said in more resigned tones, "that yeh must have them back. But I'll need to uncover them at home first. I'm not altogether sure where precisely I've concealed them in the house. But yeh can be sure yer kinsfolk in Wales will not hear tell of it, least not as long as we adhere to our agreed plan."

"How you do go on about Wales, Michael," sighed Lucy. "I'm no more Welsh than *you* are, or than Queen Adelaide for that matter. I'm *Irish* don't forget."

"I know, I know. Anyway, I'll dig them out for yeh and send them hither in due course."

"In due course, Michael?" she queried. "And how exactly am I supposed to interpret that?"

"However yeh like. I'll get them to yeh as early as yeh deserve," he answered evasively.

That the letters may be withheld indefinitely was the inference she drew from the communication. With another look of utter disdain at Miss Devereux the former Mayor grabbed his hat, drew away towards the hallway and then, with one last admonishing sigh and a look of bristling indignation, went out from her presence slamming the door loud.

Two days later when Hendrick had, by intricate representations, uncovered the true cause of Lucy's frigidity towards him, the distrust he'd harboured for his most assiduous business rival spiralled into a frenzied hatred of the man. Thus he called his foreman into the office to consult with him on a scheme that,

Hendrick calculated, would spell the utter ruin of Ferguson. Emboldened by his disdain for his business rival, Hendrick revealed a plan that would surely spell that man's downfall.

"Jacob," he began resolutely, "the town o' Castlebridge isn't big enough for both me and th'other lad, are yeh wit' me? Sure it's hardly more than an o'ergrown village to most people. Now, hear me Jacob. We take a gamble on the weather this autumn, do yeh follow? We buy in such quantities as will fill the barns to burstin' point, then sell off as to confound the markets. All even-handed and above board of course. But we bankrupt the knave before he snuffs us out, are yeh wit' me?"

"Aye it's an option for us, and certain to succeed if we're fortunate," concurred Jacob. "But is it all not a little hasty, I mean a little too venturesome for us? What if we fail in the task or the skies take an unexpected turn we'd not allowed for? Wouldn't our folly be laid bare for all to mock at?"

"It is wisdom, Jacob my friend, not folly for we don't cling to false hope. I'll not take a bet that's open to mere chance. Oh no, not if my name is Michael Hendrick. Don't yeh be noisin' it abroad Jacob but I intend to make the short trip across the river and there to consult with Mr. Furlong."

Hendrick was shrewdly aware of the marked effect that weather conditions would perennially bring to bear on the price of barley—for a wet harvest could well nigh treble it, a dry and sultry one reduce it as swiftly. The Tories had imposed severe levels of duty on the import of foreign grain. In a dry harvest, the Whig-leaning millers and barley-merchants drove hard bargains out of the land-hoarding Tory farmers. But roles were reversed in a wet autumn as the punitive import tariffs choked supply and sent domestic grain prices soaring. So Hendrick doggedly set out on his course by first procuring the counsel of a local weather-seer. The seer's name was Bill Furlong. He lived some half-mile or so west of the River Slaney, in a small old-fashioned sort of cottage up an obscure laneway near a town-land by the name of Glynn.

Mystery and intrigue hung all about this cottage, and the man himself was aloof and unfathomable. What's more, the business carried on in the place was regarded as secretive, sortilegious and occult. The innocent children of the county would squint their eyes and stop their ears whenever a 'tale of Bill Furlong' was told them. It was typically a story of some niggardly young farmer who had neglected to pay the customary fee for the prophet's solicitations only to catch his toe on a rock and fall headlong into the River Slaney to be gnawed alive by rats. Or perhaps it was of some other unfortunate soul who had fallen prey to the seemingly theurgical forces at work in the place. Now it must be distinctly understood that Michael Hendrick was not a particularly superstitious man. What drew him into this shadowy business, in addition to his own desperation to secure the downfall of Ferguson by any means at his disposal, was the remarkable reputation that Furlong appeared to own for predicting the weather with uncanny accuracy.

And so it was that one balmy night in the middle of August, Hendrick clandestinely set out for the cottage of this famed wizard. Having crossed the river at Deep's Bridge, he then trudged his way southward until he happened upon what appeared to be the domicile he'd sought. He forced open the rusty, creaking gate—sufficiently disturbing the darkness to elicit loud remonstrance from a screech owl who'd perched in a nearby tree. He was then rather startled to descry, sitting on a mound of what looked like dried dung, an old hag dressed in the most unsightly rags imaginable. The infamous old soup woman at the Wellingtonbridge Fair seemed, by comparison, a princess. This termagant had a hideously bloodcurdling face that was covered with what seemed like a crude combination of mud and slime and spittle. Her toothless slobbering mouth was odious to the senses, the harsh and cackling sound of her ghastly screeching voice was nauseating in the extreme, and she stank.

"Is this the cottage of Bill Furlong?" enquired Hendrick, not being a man to be frightened even by such abominable sights as these. The woman took a sharp intake of breath and then answered the visitor in a distinctly unfamiliar accent that seemed to originate in some rural part of southern England.

"Oh aye, aye oh aye, that it be, sir, that it be," shrieked the beldam holding a bony, shrivelled finger over her face to point in the general direction of the cottage.

"*Yes it is!*" exhorted Hendrick reproachfully, "not '*that it be*'. Good Gad, was it raised in some class o' cesspool yeh were that yeh use such foul phrases as those? Beguile me no longer y'aul' wretch, I'm off to speak to Furlong."

At first glance, the exterior of Furlong's cottage seemed less mysterious than Hendrick had been lead to expect. Indeed, it could have been any modest dwelling place in any lane in rural Wexford only for the large round hedge that seemed to encircle it from every angle. A low tunnel connecting the front garden with the porch had been strategically carved out of this hedge. It was long, dark, narrow and sloped downwards. Being a rather tall man, he stooped slightly as he passed under the arch. Groping his way down the tunnel he proceeded towards the door.

Before he had even knocked, Furlong came out to the porch. To Hendrick's mild surprise and relief, there was nothing particularly thaumaturgical about the man's appearance. His continually smoking a pipe gave any newcomers the impression that the seer was a rather pensive and contemplative individual, which indeed he was. If there was one thing capable of unnerving a visitor unaccustomed to his company however, it was in his manner of speaking. For Bill Furlong spoke in a low, soft, sluggish sort of voice. Syllables were elongated for no obvious reason and the prophet's eyes assumed a sort of staring aspect, discomforting to many, whenever he spoke of matters on which he was considered an authority.

"So, Mr. Furlong," began Hendrick, "folks tell me that it's here the farmers call when they're in need of knowin' the weather. Am I right? Y'are somewhat proven in such matters, are yeh not?"

"Eh, well now, I can tell it for y'alright, oh yeh, dependin' that is on how much y'are in need of it if yeh take my meanin'."

"Well, of course!" asserted Hendrick casting two shillings into the man's lap forthwith. After this Hendrick was invited into the cottage which, although modest, was every bit as cosy for it.

"Ah now, *two* shillin' sir. Y'are liberal to be sure. It's often only the wan I get from the farmers yeh know, or a half-crown if they're kind to me, oh yes sir, perhaps they'd come back with a tanner after the clouds are true to me, oh aye."

"Well, what can yeh do for me?" enquired Hendrick glancing eagerly at the seer.

"Ah well, sir, yeh see, I can do nottin' to change the clouds for yeh y'understand. It's only predictin' what they'll do that I'm at."

"Fine by me Furlong. Now what's it to be? Y'ave yer two shillin', now give me my two weeks. Th'outlook for harvest is what I'm after."

"D'yever carry on business with Farmer Dor'n?" asked Furlong closing one eye and glaring fixedly at Hendrick with the other.

"Farmer Dor'n of Edermine? Oh, many times, he's a regular at the Castlebridge market. Not every Saturda' mind yeh but a regular none the less."

"Yeh, well," continued Furlong, "it was him who was here this last evenin' and askin' the very same he was, 'the harvest fortnight' he said, 'what's the county in for?' oh aye, the very same fortnight."

"Good, yes, well what did yeh tell the man?" queried Hendrick perceiving all this idle banter to be a waste of both of their valuable times. Furlong rounded his lips, leant forward and almost whispered his prediction to his client.

"The first two weeks o' the month," he began, "brings forth an unrelentin' torrent, wan as will smite th'earth with downpours, oh aye the likes o' which have ne'er been seen at the Wexford harvest. Oh no, my generous friend, there'll be no sprinkles or showers in *them* two weeks, none of it sir, but a deluge somethin' terrible. And pity 'pon them that's at sea, oh yes, for squall and blizzard will beat 'pon their vessels and cast them on the mercy o' the high waters. Oh yes sir, it's nottin' but clouds and floods and blasts for fourteen long and tortuous days, make no mistake, the first two weeks o' the month mind yeh, the very first two, or my name's not Bill Furlong."

Hendrick bowed to the man's oracular authority. For many leagues around it was well known, yet rarely admitted, that the higher the fee paid for this curious man's solicitations the more startlingly accurate those same forecasts turned out to be. Hendrick rose, thanked the prophet for his services and left the cottage. The haggard old woman, the pleasure of whose company the barley-merchant had been treated to on his arrival, remained on her dung heap. She laughed at him with an evil, squeaking voice and he flung a coin at her out of some mad charitable fancy that seemed to take him just then.

"Ah, there y'are y'aul' witch, a tanner for yeh to shut that gob o' yours."

Fortunately for Hendrick, there remained three more Saturdays in August that year. On his walk back to Castlebridge he resolved to buy up as much barleycorn on the next two as he could possibly manage. All this was to allow for the possibility of Furlong's predicted downpours arriving a couple of days prematurely.

The cloudy yet relatively dry weather kept grain prices reasonably stable throughout the remainder of August. The very equivocal nature of the skies that month kept the expectations of farmers and corn-dealers alike far from the extremes of confidence and paranoia. They simply refused to speculate on what September would bring them. This incertitude was reflected on every market day.

"Looks like it's neither a buyer's *nor* a seller's market this year, Mr. Hendrick," offered Jacob as Friday drew to its close and rumours of the next day's barley prices circulated about the town.

"*That*, my friend, is where y'are wrong," retorted Hendrick with great deliberation. "Yel keep this to yerself I know but Furlong's after predictin' the most apocalyptic conditions for the first two weeks o' September. He says, Jacob, we're in for a harvest the likes o' which has ne'er been seen in Wexford. I didn't give him two bob for nottin' yeh know, ha, we're onto somethin' here Jacob.

Now hear me out. I'm after speakin' t'aul' Sweetman at the bank below. He says he'll advance us for the wan month. We've got the mill and the barns and all for security. I've even put up me own home. Now let's get to it in the mornin' Jacob. We buy like it's the last day, y'understand? Like it's the last day! No holdin' back this weekend Jacob, nor the next. Sweetman says we can pay him back the third Monda' in September. I make that the fifteenth, by which time we'll have sold off all the grain again at the lofty rates they'll fetch in such weather and have squeezed out Ferguson or hurt his trade badly at the least. We'll have the means to pay off aul' Sweetman with lots to spare. Ha, what a plan, Jacob, eh, what a plan?"

The weather continued to be temperate, prices likewise. In fact these very non-descript conditions persisted through the next two Saturdays, keeping prices moderate throughout. The last Saturday in August, being the penultimate day of the month, clouds of a rather murky and foreboding nature started to gather over Leinster. Hendrick rose early that morning, scarcely able to contain his excitement. As he well expected, he was greeted at market by the news that barley prices has started to rise a little. He and Jacob discussed details of their strategy, and Hendrick recalled in his mind the assuredness with which Furlong had foreseen the harsh tempest that now seemed only days away, if not hours. He ordered Jacob to buy up every last grain he possibly could before close of market, albeit at prices that were slightly inflated on the previous two Saturdays.

"Buy it all!" he enjoined his foreman. "Don't forsake a dram o' the stuff, d'yeh hear? For a week from now 'twill be as gold to us. Use up the bank's allowance, Jacob, to the last brass farthin' of it!"

"As you say, sir," complied Jacob.

By close of market on that last Saturday in August, very nearly one quarter of all the barleycorn in the whole of County Wexford belonged to Michael Hendrick. His barns were of course beyond bursting point. Much of the extra grain he needed to store in his own house on Codd's Walk and, although this would be inconvenient for a time, it would serve as a constant reminder of the extent to which he was to damage his biggest rival in the barley business. Anywhere there was indoor space, such that was free from rats and pilferers, immense quantities of grain were severally stashed. Even Jacob was called upon to store two or three dozen barrels at his own home wherever contiguous space could be found. He lived far closer to the mill than did Hendrick, his meagre cottage lying to the east of the town just at the corner of Dixon Lane and the Blackwater Road.

One of the most prominent farmers in Leinster—let alone Wexford—was Jimmy Dempsey of Scurlocksbush, with whom Jacob placed an order for six hundred and twenty barrels of barley. Dempsey had quoted his new barley at a competitive £1.15.0 a barrel. Yet owing to the sheer magnitude of the order, Jacob had succeeded in haggling the price down to £1.12.4 a barrel.

"Yeh say y'are after *six hundred and twenty barrels*?" said the farmer incredulously. "It's a quare big load o' greeyan. Still, it can be got for yeh." Dempsey fumbled around with a piece of paper for few moments, scratched his head, fingered his beard, fumbled again, then scratched his head again. "Y'are talkin' a tousand pound wort' o' barley here Jacob. I've no boddur gettin' pickers if it's payin' me up front yel be."

Jacob seized the farmer's hand and shook it reassuringly. The deal was concluded. Though such vast quantities of grain were within Dempsey's capacity to produce, neither party had access to the forty-eight wagons and the ninety-six horses required to transport the produce to Castlebridge from Dempsey's ubiquitously located barns. Jacob consulted with his master. He then had to make the rather embarrassing request that the supplier hold off on actually transporting the produce itself to Castlebridge, expatiating that Hendrick would either send for it when room became available or would inform a third party of its whereabouts when sold on.

His neighbours and friends in the town watched this pandemonium with awe and wonder. Locals marvelled at rumours that Nancy Muckridge, Simon Lowney and Christy Colfer were being handsomely paid for taking it in turns to guard the courtyard against rats and other unwelcome visitors that might threaten the wholeness of the produce in hand. Hendrick patted Jacob on the back, tossed him a couple of extra shillings for "th'extra effort yeh put in," and repaired to his house for the night.

The following morning Hendrick awoke to the sound of constant, yet not particularly violent, precipitation. Drawing back the curtains to be greeted by damp, sodden, overcast weather was never so pleasant to any man as it was to Hendrick this last morning in August. Even as the good folks of the town poured out of their several dwelling places for the weekly walk to church—either on Ardcavan Road or Gorey Road, depending on their respective allegiances—the cries of "bad day", "wet aul' mornin'" and "quare damp Sunda'" could be heard amidst the throng. But the day was anything but bad for Hendrick. This demonstrated the universal neutrality of weather, being something which can be deemed to be a blessing or a curse depending on one's own individual, therefore subjective, purposes. To a dealer who seemed to own every grain of barleycorn in about three baronies, it seemed a most propitious of starts to the harvest season. The former Mayor believed he had backed a good horse.

To his utter astonishment, Hendrick awoke the following morning to a powerfully dazzling beam of sunlight that all but entirely illuminated his east-facing bedroom.

"Must be a little blip, I suppose," he muttered to himself drawing back the curtains with a good deal less alacrity than the previous morning. "Sure 'twill turn foul again I'm sure."

If the weather had been pleasantly bright that morning, at least it was not actually warm and Hendrick could detect that unmistakable cool freshness so characteristic of an early September dawn. This was a source of consolation as far as it went. The merchant also had time on his side for, despite the various comings and goings at the mill on a weekday, the wholesale buying and selling of barleycorn invariably took place on Saturdays.

But by mid-week the weather had gone from being bright and pleasant to being positively warm, sultry even. By Saturday a cloud was not to be seen in the sky for miles. It was stone-splittingly hot for the time of year, in consequence of which barley prices plummeted. As if circumstances had not contrived against Hendrick's plan enough, there seemed no end in sight as the entire county basked in what appeared to be an Indian summer. Tragically for Hendrick, this brilliant sunshine continued for another full week. On the eve of the second Saturday in September, Hendrick stood in his office in uncontrollable rage.

"Curse that *scoundrel* of a weather seer!" he shouted thumping his large hand against the office wall. "I'll give *him* storm and tempest when I get my hands on him. The rogue's all but bankrupted me."

"Curious, Michael," stuttered Jacob nervously, "he's never been that wrong before I'm sure. It's a bad call and no mistake."

This understatement brought a stern glance from Hendrick that silenced his foreman. The following day was one of the most painful of Michael Hendrick's entire life. He was required to sell off every last grain of his barleycorn. This manoeuvre, given the embarrassingly low prices in such a depressed market, only part-settled his debt with the bank. He had purchased when the grain was priced at anything up to £2 a barrel. Such prices, though not particularly low, would have more than doubled were Furlong's prophecies fulfilled. As it happened, Hendrick arrived at the corn exchange that second Saturday in September to learn that prices had dropped considerably.

Saturday mornings at the corn exchange proceeded thus. A huge blackboard was erected at one end of the room. Across the top was inscribed the various categories of produce being traded, with three large columns under each. The sub-headings consisted of the letters 'L', 'S' and 'D'—denoting pounds, shillings and pence respectively. Listed down the left hand side of the blackboard were the surnames of the local traders, each row containing the prices that said merchant was currently charging for his produce.

As was his wont, Hendrick arrived early at the exchange that morning. He had always taken note of market fluctuations, but today he fastidiously tracked every change in the prices quoted under 'Barley'. To his utter dismay the sub-column headed 'L' contained the digit '1' from top to bottom. One reputable merchant with whom Hendrick had conducted much business over the years was Freddie Lacey of Skreen. Lacey's barley began the day at £1.1.6—a mere three pence higher than Hendrick's own price. As temperatures rose and it became evident that the county was being treated to yet another scorcher, prices deflated to an unprecedented level. Hendrick withdrew to the outer court and shook his fist at the sun. The primary object of his wrath was in the southern sky, yet Hendrick's fist seemed inclined marginally to the southwest, as if drawn subconsciously in the direction of a certain cottage at Glynn. As Castlebridge baked in a fierce heat and the locals wiped their swarthy visages, Hendrick cursed the heavens defiantly.

At twelve noon, Timmy Busher of Oylegate clenched his fist and obliterated from the chart his own barley price of £1.0.3 a barrel only to chalk up a revised asking price of £0.19.6 a barrel. An important psychological threshold had been burst. The price of new barley had crashed below the £1 mark for the first time in living memory. Panic set in around the exchange as other merchants hastily followed suit. As the searing sun promised an abundant harvest, that same tropical weather had Hendrick cornered. His only option was to indulge in an exercise of damage limitation. He must sell off before prices sank any lower. But his flooding the market in so short a period of time had the immediate effect of slashing the prices yet further. By three o'clock that afternoon, Hendrick was forced to sell off his last remaining barleycorn at a paltry ten shillings a barrel.

Had he wrongly speculated on the harvest weather with reasonable quantities of produce, then his losses would have been smarting enough. But as he had acquired such vast quantities in eager anticipation of higher prices, his losses were catastrophic in the extreme. The weekend passed. Then Monday arrived and, with it, fresh uncertainties. Gloomily strolling from the bank towards his milling complex, having been advised that both the latter *and* Slaneyview House were now officially the property of that bank, Hendrick was in no mood for the news that greeted him.

It seemed that Ferguson, who had exercised restraint during August, had been buying up sedulously that very weekend. Barley had never been so cheap. When indulging in market speculation, success hinged on but three considerations—timing, timing and timing. Ferguson's was impeccable. In one particular transaction he'd bought six barrels from Timmy Busher and had still received change from a £3 note. Hendrick cringed. As if such news wasn't afflictive enough, a conversation with his foreman later that afternoon all but propelled the former Mayor into a profound state of desperation.

"In that consultation in Furlong's cottage," said Jacob with inquisitive undertones, "did either party actually mention the word 'September' at any time?"

"What's that to do with anythin'?" replied Hendrick gruffly. "Why yeh can't be tellin' me he was ont'October. Even seers can't predict the conditions *that* far ahead."

"Oh, it's true, Michael, very true that, they can't," conceded Jacob, "but y'asked him for the 'harvest fortnight', yeh?"

"That's it Jacob, the 'harvest fortnight', now what are yeh gettin' at?"

"Well, when Furlong gave his prediction, was it by any chance for the 'first fortnight of the month'? Were them his exact words?"

"That was pretty much the extent of it, but is it wastin' my time y'are at or is there a point to this? I'm losin' patience wit' yeh Jacob, what are y'onta?"

"Don't be gettin' fashed with me, Michael, but I believe I can account for our unfortunate miscalculation," said Jacob soberly. "Bein' yer first ever time at a weather-seer, I sort of assumed yed o' done a little research into the business before jumpin' in wit' both feet. It's clear to me now that yeh didn't, and it's after spellin' the downfall o' this barley business o' yours. Yeh see, Michael, ordinary folks like us talk about months as they're named in the year. But a seer, ah now, he's a different animal from us. For the seer reads the winds and the skies and the moon. The *moon*, Michael, get it? The *moon*! A seer's *'month'* is always lunar and it seems yeh were ignorant of it."

Hendrick folded his arms, stared across the table at his foreman with a daunting expression and spoke directly to him.

"And when exactly, my useful friend, is the next new moon supposed to rise for us, hmm?" he enquired.

"Well by my reckonin' it's tomorrow night, about ten o'clock I'd say. Yeh, best guess about ten tomorrow night," replied Jacob nodding.

"Ten tomorrow night, hmm?" repeated Hendrick gritting his teeth with half-suppressed rage.

It was not yet seven on that Monday night in mid-September yet it seemed particularly dark even for the time of year, a season when lighted hours shorten by the day. The two men sat staring at each other for a few more moments and this was rather disconcerting to Jacob. He felt vulnerable being gazed at in such a sombre manner, and stirred visibly.

Suddenly a blinding flash illuminated the entire courtyard, much of the intense light penetrating the office within. This was followed several seconds later by a distant rumble. The two men continued to stare across the table at each other as if no words were necessary. Another bright flash followed by another booming rumble, this time louder and less delayed. They could hear the patter of hail beginning to fall without, and doing so with growing intensity. Both men got to their feet. Eager to get a fair glimpse at the heavens, the two then tore across the office and jostled for position at its modest Georgian window. Owing to his superior physical strength, it was Hendrick who triumphed in that particular tussle. Even as he did so, another blindingly intense bolt of fork lightening tore a crevice in the sky. It was the third of many. There then followed the most ferocious and cataclysmic thunderstorm that was ever witnessed in the model county. Huge pellets of hail incessantly and unremittingly belted down upon every street and upon every roof and, to the dismay of many a farmer, upon every field. It was a torrent that none could withstand and that nothing would attenuate. Any crops yielded by the earth but as yet ungathered were utterly devastated. The remainder of the season was an unmitigated washout, leaving many farmers distraught at its intensity.

This violent barrage of hail and rain and sleet upon the earth lasted a full twelve days. Enormous hailstones intemperately smote the ground that autumn. Their velocity was rivalled only by that with which the price of barley proceeded in the opposite direction. *It* soared to unprecedented levels. Grain that Hendrick had bought for nearly £2 a barrel—and had subsequently sold for ten shillings—now fetched prices of up to £6. Shrewd business mind as he was blessed with, Ferguson was selling. And doing so at ostentatious margins. Aided by his percipient reading of the market, the so-called 'Kingstown Upstart' had struck gold. Hendrick, meanwhile, had gambled and had lost disastrously.

CHAPTER 14

❦

A Couple of Days Off

September had passed and October was waning when Hendrick resolved to renew his fervent representations to Lucy Devereux. Now, more than ever, he had reason for doing so with fresh vigour and purpose. The man was reeling after his ill-judged speculation on the recent harvest and was acutely aware that the day of the bank's foreclosure on Slaneyview House could not be long delayed. Time was of the essence. Were Lucy Devereux to agree to his demands and take him as her husband, then it would seem the most obvious course for them both to live securely at Oldtown Manor.

Uncertain as he was of the precise date that the bank would prescribe for the repossession, Hendrick set about diligently retrieving every last epistle that had been sent him from his former lover during that twenty-four year period. These were gathered together from various locations around the house but the majority of them had been safely stowed in the nether regions of his attic, well concealed from the wandering eyes of either of the two women whom he had of late sheltered under his roof.

One particular Friday evening he sat in his large dining room sifting through those letters, re-reading them and arranging them in chronological order. Their directness and candour were even more striking than he had remembered. He would wrap them securely, seal the wrapping and store them in a location whence they could be readily retrieved. But he would hold off on sending the parcel over to Oldtown Manor just yet. Hendrick knew full well that he held an ace. He was conscious of the risk to his own reputation and was genuinely reluctant to damage Lucy's without cause, but there was a menacing streak in this man's nature that prompted him to play this powerfully influential hand for all that it was worth.

His course was set. He resolved to intimidate his former lover with implicit threats that some or all of her letters of passion may negligently fall into the hands of Robert Ferguson. The woman would feel desperately compromised and would be cajoled into marrying Hendrick. At the very least, the threat of their being publicised would force her hand in responding unfavourably to any offer of marriage from Ferguson. The first outcome would achieve his plan's primary ambition, the second would at least satisfy the perverted cravings of this man's deep-rooted and chronic insecurities.

If there was one innocent bystander amidst the incertitude that pervaded the lives of both Lucy Devereux and Michael Hendrick that autumn, then it was the latter's stepdaughter Megan-Leanne. Having so lately found real happiness for the very first time in her life this young princess had been stripped of the primary source of that contentment—Mr. Robert Ferguson, the poaching of whom was at the hands of a queen to which it seemed she herself could not hold a candle.

Despite her simple nature, Megan carried around with her a curious pessimism that enabled her to 'bear the slings and arrows of outrageous fortune' as though they were nothing more than her lot in life. Enigmatically, the same young girl admitted good fortune and blessing as though *they* were little more than her deserts. This rather dynamic indifference to providence, though seasoned with a principled sensitivity to right and wrong, had enabled her supplanting by her mistress as Ferguson's sweetheart to occur almost seamlessly. It took place without any rancour between the two women, without their friendship being soured and without either person becoming embittered as a consequence of it. Megan-Leanne knew her station in life. To be middle class was, on the social ladder of the day, to be a whole rung below that of Lucy Devereux.

"You seem a little disheartened this last while, Miss Devereux," observed Megan over breakfast one morning. "Is there something that's troubling you? Remember that I came to you for friendship as well as service. It's something that my father said to you isn't it? He can be so heated sometimes."

"Oh Megan, you're the kindest of maidens," replied Lucy gratefully yet sombrely. "It's just Castlebridge, Megan. The town is getting under my skin right now. I came here without knowing a sinner in the place. I'm still not well known amongst the townsfolk despite being born and bred in the county. Most consider themselves beneath me and remain aloof, knowing me to be a moneyed lady. You know what folks are like, Megan, all tish and bother in such matters when there's really no call for it."

Lucy Devereux sighed. Megan perceived that the real cause of her mistress's melancholy just then was the notable absence of Robert Ferguson, who'd gone into the country to negotiate some hay-deal or other. It certainly was. But Lucy recoiled from openly admitting this to one who'd so recently enjoyed that suitor's affections. Both women regarded Castlebridge as a drab, empty and purposeless place without him, but neither admitted it to the other. In her meditative gloom, Lucy took a deep breath and continued.

"I have decided, Megan my dear, that I am in need of a short break in the country. I must go somewhere remote and pleasant, somewhere without the hustle and noisome exchanges of a busy market town. I have a friend of many years who lives near to Carne Beach. Carne really is a most delightful of seclusions Megan, you must pay it a visit one day. She has kindly written inviting me to stay awhile. I shall only be away for four days or so. Hartley will attend to your needs and I trust you will rather enjoy being mistress of Oldtown Manor for a time. Should you wish to contact me on anything pressing, I shall write the name and address of my friend on a piece of paper ere I depart."

With that Lucy Devereux raised herself from her chair, proceeded to her study and returned with a pen and a small piece of paper. She took some seconds to write a few lines on it and then handed it to Megan-Leanne. Megan regarded the name and address written thereon.

Miss Lucy Devereux
c/o Miss Yvonne Rossiter
Carna Manor
Carne
Barony of Forth

Megan-Leanne often conjectured on whether her mistress enjoyed any acquaintance with persons living in domiciles that were anything other than manorial. This inscription served little to mitigate those speculations.

A couple of days later, the tall and well-built figure of Michael Hendrick could be seen striding purposefully up the long gravelled drive of Oldtown Manor. It was the last weekend in October and the dense fog that hung all around the manor lent to it a kind of medieval ambiance for a time.

"I'm afraid mistress is out of town for a few days sir, being away in the country," said Hartley as he answered the large front door of the manor. "I can see whether Miss Hendrick is disposed just now if you like?"

"Eh, well," hesitated Hendrick, "yes, eh, yes I'd very much like to speak with young Miss Hendrick if it's convenient."

"Very well, sir."

Hendrick stood in the large opulently decorated hallway of the manor for some minute or two and regarded once more the huge and expensive paintings that bedecked it. The servant returned promptly and ushered Hendrick into the manor's library.

"Oh, father," cried Megan jovially and slamming closed a small dusty book she had just been engrossed in, "so nice of you to call and see me." She embraced her stepfather affectionately and kissed him twice.

"Well," said Michael glancing around at the numerous shelves, "impressive collection your mistress seems to have. I never knew she'd so many books under her roof."

"But how *would* you, father?" remarked Megan confidently. "You've only known the woman since she moved to Castlebridge a few months back, and you've only been to see us a handful of times since, what with all your grain dealings and such in the harvest."

"Well, it's true Megan dear, it's true," Hendrick rejoined with decent resignation, "but yeh know how she's so much more acceptin' o' the professional classes than most of her ilk. Sure I sometimes nearly forget she's a lady at all. Look at her keepin' company with that Ferguson chap now, oh ha, a little below her station don't yeh think?"

"Some would have said that mother was a little below *yours*," replied Megan unexpectedly. "But let's not dwell on such matters," she continued partly regretting the comment.

"Yeh know somethin' Megan, I'm heartily sorry that yer own liaison with Ferguson never blossomed into somethin'. Oh, yes, heartily sorry for *both* yer sakes."

"But I thought you and he were business rivals father," enquired Megan bemused at his sentiments. "Would it not be a bitter pill for you to give him the hand of your only daughter in marriage?"

Hendrick shrugged his shoulders and replied in the negative. He then proceeded to assure his stepdaughter that it was *her* interests he had at heart and that, if anything, to marry a shrewd and prosperous barley-dealer such as Ferguson could only bring fortune, security and comfort to the girl. These considerations were of course not at all the driving motives behind his eagerness to see their romance revived, though whether or not his stepdaughter's simple imagination had permitted her to realise this fact Hendrick did not as yet perceive.

"He's a masher to be sure. Are yeh not a little grieved that he's givin' his attentions to yer mistress instead o' yerself?" continued Hendrick seeming to ignore her earlier appeals to abandon the topic.

"I accept it father, as I must," she replied equably. "There's no doubting he's of good breeding and does seem to have a head for business. Perhaps he's just found 'metal more attractive'."

Hendrick was unfamiliar with the simile. Yet noticing that Megan had just replaced the book she'd been reading into a box-set superscribed *"The Complete Works of William Shakespeare"*, he guessed well its likely originator.

"The butler tells me Lucy's after goin' away for a time?" continued Hendrick.

"That's right, she has decided to spend a few days at Carne Beach with her good friend Miss Rossiter. It would appear that Miss Devereux has a lot on her mind at the moment."

"*Carne Beach?*" exclaimed Hendrick, sounding rather startled.

"Yes," replied his stepdaughter. "What is so unusual about that? It sounds a most pretty of resorts and just the medicine that mistress needs right now."

"It's just that," mused Hendrick, "I seen Lucy with me own eyes a couple o' days back. She was travellin' in her chaise and carried a little luggage with her, all o' which indeed suggested a sojourn o' some class. As a result I was not altogether surprised when Hartley told me she'd gone away for a few days. But what's so puzzlin' is that, from my own house, I seen Lucy leavin' the town along Codd's Walk and that leads *westward* towards Crossabeg. If it's Carne Beach she was off to then why not th'Ardcavan Road? She's a woman o' means as we know and the toll at Wexford Bridge would be as nottin' to such as her. She's off to Carne Beach and her carriage drives along *westward*? There's somethin' she's not tellin' yeh Megan. There surely is. It's quare as news from Bree."

The direction in which Lucy's carriage had driven out of Castlebridge was in fact something of which Megan-Leanne was entirely ignorant, this despite her stepfather's harbouring suspicions to the contrary. Her mistress had not deemed it necessary to volunteer such information to the girl. Furthermore, the interchange of Ardcolm Road with Ardcavan Road, just at the southern end of Castlebridge, was comprehensively obscured from the view of anyone within the confines of Oldtown Manor. This fact owed to the several hundred yards that separated the two locations as well as to the density of the arborescence that stood betwixt them.

"Be that as it may," replied Megan, "she's gone and will be away for another day or two."

"Very well," sighed Hendrick, hands on hips. "I'll call again I suppose. But yeh should be gettin' back courtin' with that Ferguson chap again. He's the fella for yeh Megan and no mistake. Bye for now."

Megan wished him well and resumed her reading. She was puzzled by the eagerness and fervour on the part of her father, or so she called him, to have the alliance with Ferguson rekindled. Continuing in her studies of Shakespeare, the words *'doth protest too much methinks'* leaped up from the page with surprising aptness.

CHAPTER 15

❀

A Reversal of Fortunes

The real motivation for Lucy's departing Castlebridge by its western road was simple. It was indeed her very intention to be observed proceeding along Codd's Walk. This would inevitably lead to that same thoroughfare being diligently watched in eager anticipation of her return. She could then arrive discreetly, unchecked, to her abode in the southeast of the town, doing so by making the return journey quietly over Wexford Bridge and Ardcavan Road. And so she did.

All the while Hendrick sat at home gloomily considering what schemes could be contrived to delay the foreclosure on Slaneyview House, his business at the mill being already in the receivership of the bank. Having mused on it for some time, this resourceful if impatient man conceived of one possible course that remained open to him. He immediately put pen to paper and craftily worded a further correspondence to be delivered, with all manner of haste, to one 'Miss Lucy Devereux of Oldtown Manor'.

Dear Lucy,

On calling to the manor some two days ago, I was informed by your servant that you had removed yourself to the country for a short break. I was further informed by Megan that it was at Carne Beach you were staying.

I trust that, in your wisdom, you will have afforded yourself a little time to consider my renewed offer. There is nothing in the world, my dear Lucy, which should hinder our betrothal one to the other. Yet I'll leave the date of the wedding and all such matters in your capable hands. I'll not mind when it happens, Lucy, as long as we're to wed. One small favour I'd ask of you in the meantime. You're aware that a foreclosure is pending on Slaneyview House. All I'd ask you to do is call at the bank with me next week and talk to Sweetman. We can tell him we're promised to each other and we're to be married next year. This will surely forestall the repossession. Even if we've not set a date for it, he'll hold off when he learns that I'm to be marrying such a woman of property as yourself. There can be no doubting it Lucy. Can't you do this for me? Won't you do it?

One other matter, I have finally accomplished the business of retrieving every last one of your letters to me. Yes, Lucy, they're safe and discreet where none will uncover them. If you're agreed on our plan to visit Mr. Sweetman, I can take the parcel with me to the bank and there hand it over to you, either to destroy or to do with as you please. There can't be a better plan than this. Yours is the next move. To quote your own letter of earlier this year, 'may the day be not too long delayed'.

Yours,

Mr. Michael Hendrick
Slaneyview House
Codd's Walk.

Now it was widely known that Lucy Devereux and Yvonne Rossiter enjoyed the closest and most trusting of affinities. They had been bosom friends since childhood, and their conviviality one to the other was unrivalled in the county. Miss Rossiter's people had, in fact, hailed from just outside Castlebridge but had lived for some time in Adamstown, the village where Lucy was born. In those days, folk were socially compartmentalised by more than mere class, station, or level of wealth. There existed another method by which one could readily draw a line of division through any rural community, namely along the lines of its inhabitants' ecclesiastical allegiances.

Given that a person's individual religious persuasion was in those days no small matter of indifference, many folks marvelled at the unparalleled rapport that existed between two women from such diametrically opposite traditions. Indeed the bonds of their friendship were so strong that each had on occasion attempted to win the other over to 'the true faith', loath as she was to contemplate the utterly hopeless fate that otherwise awaited her heretical friend in the next life. Waggish remarks that her friend would be warmly welcomed into 'the Christian family' met with retorts of a similarly proselytising nature.

But in spite of the concern that each woman affectionately displayed for the eternal spiritual welfare of her dear companion, their staunch devotion to the church of their respective family background paradoxically yielded enormous benefits to the twain in this life. For in addition to the implied trust that existed between them, it was always tacitly understood that the life of each woman would rarely, if ever, have occasion to overlap with an ordained member of her friend's community. This was especially relevant for Miss Rossiter, whose family seemed to provide its church with a disproportionately high number of its clergy.

Thus the two women kept no secret one from the other, confident that neither would arrive in church the following Sunday only to be denounced from the pulpit of the most heinous and unforgivable crime of falling helplessly in love with a member of the opposite sex, and further of the unspeakable sin of sharing moments of intimacy with him. Had the two women attended the same church and worshipped there as sisters sharing a common faith, the chances of any such personal details being publicised would have been extremely low. But their divided religious loyalties ensured that the chances were zero. Thus they withheld nothing from each other. Lucy Devereux had called on her friend in desperate need of advice.

The former Mayor, impatient in all matters as he was, did not have to wait long for a reply to his letter. Having assiduously kept watch over Codd's Bridge against the lady's return, fruitless as such vigilance was destined to be, he was pleasantly surprised when a letter arrived. It was directed in Lucy's quaint handwriting and ran to three full pages. Letter writing was Lucy's favourite pastime. Just as well that paper, though prohibitively expensive to most, was in ready supply at Oldtown Manor.

Dear Michael,

Thank you for your recent correspondence. Buffeted as I felt by the pace of life at Castlebridge, not to mention your cloaked threats to deviously coax me into a union for which I had no appetite, I sought solitude in a short holiday at Carne Beach. You're no doubt aware that I stayed with my good friend and confidant Yvonne Rossiter. Miss Rossiter is one of the few true companions I have left in the world, Michael, and you'll not deny me the pleasure of a few days away. I certainly derived in that place a measure of relief from the distress and the anguish that your ardent representations had so caused in me of late.

But a quest for solitude and repose was not the chief and primary purpose of my sojourn at Carne, as you will discover when you regard how I have signed this latest epistle to you. Yes, Michael, it was while at Carne that I married Robert. I pray that you will not curse me for it. It was the only course open to me, Michael. So afraid was I that you would reveal all of our past to him and I might never enjoy his favour again, that I pledged myself to him there and then. I figured that, as long as I remained an unmarried woman, you would perceive there was a remote chance of your securing me by threats and manipulation. As long as you harboured such ambitions, I was always exposed to your blackmail and could never rest easy. This is all, of course, in addition to the undying love that I have had for Robert from the moment we met. You will, naturally, understand that there remains now no motive for you to browbeat me any longer on this matter. Such would only serve to embitter us further and would be to no avail, closed as I now am to any further entreaties of marriage.

Michael, you and I are but the ashes of our former fires. Our intimacies at Ceredigion were nigh on a quarter of a century ago. Since then you have had your chance of happiness with Susanna and, although she is now passed beyond this life, the name of Hendrick yet boasts a most beautiful and gentle of maidens in Megan-Leanne. By the way, an aunt of mine travelled from Wellingtonbridge to witness my marriage. She is Jane Whitty, a baker's widow. She alluded to a horrid rumour that a man named Hendrick had once auctioned off his wife at some local market or other in that village. Of course I refused to believe it and even defended your good name in the matter. Your sound reputation as Mayor, coupled with your unquenchable determination for us both to take the honourable course, taught me that such a man was never capable of effecting a transaction so distasteful and improper.

I was heartily sorry to learn of your being declared bankrupt. But strongly as I should be impressed with this sentiment, you will appreciate that there remains no conceivable circumstance under which I can acquiesce to your proposal to deceive Mr. Sweetman. I cannot pretend we are betrothed. Neither can I suffer you to live under my roof. I can only ensure that you'll ever find me equally disposed as you have always found me to render you every service and assistance in my power such as do my name and honour no injury.

Michael, you have already fulfilled so many of your personal ambitions in life; to marry young, to father a comely and respectable maiden, to command your own barley business and to serve as a Town Mayor. Now you must allow me my one chance at personal contentment. I beseech you, one more time, to return to me that parcel of letters you have so diligently compiled and stowed.

I wish you well and continue to trust that sound judgement will prevail.

Yours always,

Mrs. Lucy Ferguson
Oldtown Manor
Ardcolm.

Hendrick was unappeasably indignant. Never had he suspected that Lucy would return from Carne a married woman (though the marriage ceremony had taken place not at Carne itself but in the nearby parish of Horetown). This manoeuvre was far outside the scope of his perception. Had he harboured any such suspicions he would certainly have attempted, for good or ill, to disabuse her of such a fanciful notion in good time. But it was too late.

Two years earlier he'd befriended Ferguson, had furnished him employment and had confided in him. At that time, the bachelor was sympathetic. He'd learnt of a fifteen-year-old girl with whom Hendrick had been intimate many years ago on a Welsh beach. But Ferguson was, and continued to be, as ignorant of that woman's identity as Hendrick had hitherto been of the Dubliner's matrimonial ambitions.

Lucy Devereux—now 'Mrs. Ferguson'—seemed more eager than ever to effect the return of the letters that were causing her such anguish. Hendrick saw through his former lover's blandishments, yet resolved to deny her request for the present. His predicament was such that it was only a matter of days before he would be distrained of his few remaining assets. There was absolutely no choice open to him but one—he must sue for bankruptcy.

When all of this sorry business had been accomplished, Hendrick strolled solemnly and dejectedly away from the bank. As he had suspected, he found that he could not afford to rent the tasteful if modest dwelling place on Ardcavan Road that had so recently been vacated by Robert Ferguson. With a degree of incertitude then he wandered off, his few remaining possessions in his travel bag, towards the east of Castlebridge and wended his way to the cottage of Jacob, his erstwhile foreman. Happily, Jacob showed pity for the ex-Mayor and took him under his roof.

"Well, Mr. Hendrick," he said holding the front door open and admitting his former employer, "there's a small anteroom off the kitchen I use for storin' aul' bits and bobs from time to time. It's paltry enough but there's a bed and a small fireplace too for in the winter."

Embittered as Jacob was by Hendrick's earlier treatment of him, he did not have the heart to mention that this was the very room he had utilised when called upon to store some of the excess barleycorn during the pair's ill-fated speculation in the autumn. Hendrick entered the room, nodded his gratitude and unshouldered his travelling bag. The springs of his bed twanged and creaked as he moodily cast his considerable frame thereon. How had it come to this? Six months previously, he was a prosperous barley-dealer and respected Town Mayor, was all but engaged to be married to Lucy Devereux and was living in what seemed like a palace by comparison with his new chambers. Now he was a lone and downcast bankrupt that had thrown himself on the mercy of his former employee.

But salt was to be rubbed into the wound yet. Filling up the kettle to make a great big pot of tea for himself and his new tenant, Jacob ventured to remark on a sale of some properties that had taken place over the previous two days.

"Yeh," he began, "I'm sure ye've heard o' the sellin' up o' the Manor th'other day. Yeh, well 'twill be in this week's Castle & Bridge I'm sure."

"Oldtown Manor sold up?" repeated Hendrick from within his room. "Then where's Mr. and Mrs. Ferguson gone to for heaven's sake? And Megan-Leanne?"

"Well, it's said," replied Jacob bending to place his kettle over the flames, "that the happy couple are after buyin' up Slaneyview House. Not sure if yer stepdaughter's movin' in with them though. Must be smartin' a little after the hasty marriage of her mistress to her own sweetheart, don't yeh think?"

"My house and all," whispered Hendrick disconsolately, "he comes to Castlebridge, I give him a footin' in the town and he rewards me by takin' the hand of a woman that's rightly mine, drivin' me into desperate measures in the market place, measures as have me penniless today, and now he's after buyin' up my house and all. Why the fella'd steal my grave as quick."

Now Jacob's cottage was located in close proximity to the milling complex where he'd had employment of Hendrick for so many years. It was located on a corner and its aspect was such that any happenings in the general vicinity of the mill wheel were readily observable through the window of its minute living room. The only exception was whenever a large and heavily laden hay carriage was approaching or departing Castlebridge upon the Blackwater Road. Even then the view was only partially and temporarily obscured.

As both men sat pensively over their mugs of tea, Hendrick solemnly reflected on his sharp vicissitudes of fortune. Suddenly he started. He had recognised the tall and slim female figure opposite to be none other than his own stepdaughter. She appeared to be pointing towards something beyond the archway and, on passing thus into the courtyard, was lost to her stepfather's view. For the last dozen or so years, a large, tastefully designed and prominently positioned nameplate had greeted all visitors to the courtyard. It had clearly and proudly borne the inscription

"Hendrick—Miller, Merchant and Barley Dealer".

Now it must be understood that Megan-Leanne was conscious of the fact that her stepfather's business had been seized by the bank to pay off his debts. What perplexed the girl just then, and the aspect of the business that had drawn her attention to the nameplate from without the courtyard, lay not in the apparent tardiness on the part of Hendrick's creditors to remove the sign. Rather it was in their seeming to efface it instead. And to do so only partially. For about the past twenty-four hours the sign looked hopelessly asymmetrical, and read

"   —Miller, Merchant and Barley Dealer",

the notably absent word "Hendrick" having being smeared over by two coats of meticulously applied black paint. But what startled the girl even more was that the same tradesman who had been charged with removing her surname (or so she believed it to be) from the plate was standing directly in front of that same sign holding a large tin of white paint in one hand and a long thin paint brush in the other. Not wishing to stare at him for fear it was not seemly so to do, the young maiden slowly began to wander around the courtyard and search for Amos Wickham, or for Nancy Muckridge, or for any one of Hendrick's former workers with whom she was on first name terms.

For it seemed to Megan that business had continued as normal. Trusses of hay were being carried hither and thither, heavily loaded wagons were arriving and departing, and the very same workfolk that had enjoyed employment of her stepfather for so many years flitted in and out of the granaries and haybarns as busy in their rigours today as they'd ever been. After several minutes of this wandering, a large head of curly brown hair was clumsily thrust out of a third floor window of one of the granaries.

"Hey! Oi! Miss Hendrick! Is it yerself?" it called loudly. The voice was that of the inimitable Amos Wickham.

"Hush!" retorted Megan, always sensitive to public utterances of her name at such a volume. She beckoned to him to come and speak to her in the courtyard. Then turning her back towards the granary she glanced once more at the nameplate she'd been regarding some minutes earlier. To her astonishment, the painter had painstakingly drawn out four letters of the new surname under which the business was henceforth to be directed. They were an 'F', followed by an 'E', then an 'R' and finally a 'G'. The painter was beginning to artistically draw out the fifth, a letter 'U', when Wickham arrived, sweating and panting as usual.

"Well, Miss Hendrick," he said, his face all in a glow. "Is it here that yeh are?"

"Wickham," she said, ignoring his use of dialect, "the name 'Hendrick' has been erased from the plate yonder. I thought they were going to remove it and sell off the premises. But now I see there's a new name being inscribed. Has Robert Ferguson really bought out the whole concern?"

"Oh, he surely has, Miss Hendrick," confirmed Wickham, nodding profusely. "There's more property changin' hands in Castlebridge in these fair times as there was in the days of aul' Ollie Grumble. Yeh see, when Mr. Hendrick was after losin' his credit an' all and he was after bein' declared a bankrupt and what have yeh, beggin' yer pardon miss for I know he's yer stepfather an' all, but Mr. Ferguson come along and says t'us 'back to work'. He says a new sign's a waste of a guinea and why not be paintin' over th'auld wan. They say our new master's after comin' from Kingstown up Dublin way but I'm cursed if there's not somethin' o' the Scatchman in him, savin' a few bob like that!"

With that Megan-Leanne thanked Wickham and went out of the courtyard. When she told her stepfather of this news, the blood rose in his face. Jacob, too, was incensed at the news when he learnt it some minutes later. The two men's indignation was, however, owing to two vastly different reasons. For Hendrick, it seemed as if his supplanting by Ferguson was now complete. The blotting out of his surname and its replacement within hours by that of his rival's was galling to the man. For Jacob, his resentment of Ferguson stemmed from the fact that he appeared to be alone among the former employees of Hendrick that Ferguson had not re-hired at the mill. Owing to the fact that it was Ferguson who had originally supplanted him when the position of foreman was first advertised, this latest snub only served to augment his disdain for the Dubliner.

The halcyon days of winter had ushered in the festive season and a new year has been rung in when, on a wintry Thursday night in mid-January, there came a knock at the door of Slaneyview House. A servant answered it. Lucy was mildly surprised to discover the visitor was none other than Alderman Parle, the Deputy Mayor. He was dressed in a long black coat, with its collar raised to full height, and a bowler hat. He asked to speak to Mr. Ferguson at once. Lucy, who was by now standing in the hallway, welcomed him.

"He's just in the study," she confirmed. "Come in and sit by the fire or you'll catch your death on such a night."

Parle gratefully accepted and Lucy then promptly went to fetch her husband.

"It's Alderman Parle, the Deputy Mayor," she said. "He's in the dining room by the fire."

On entering the room Ferguson couldn't help but notice the rather sombre expression on the Alderman's face just then. Parle asked their pardon for disturbing them 'on such a night' but told them it was urgent business.

"You may or may not have heard, Mr. Ferguson," he began, "but Mayor Lambert passed away some two hours ago."

"Oh, I hadn't," replied Ferguson concernedly. "I'm very sorry to hear it."

"Well he'd not been well as you know. Frankly he hasn't been out of bed since before Christmas, poor fellow. Anyway, I've come here tonight to ask you if you would be willing to allow your name to go forward to succeed him. After the debacle in the summer, the Corporation are reluctant to have another contest. We've agreed on a single candidate and, if you say you're willing, will confirm you as Mayor."

"Well," replied Ferguson smiling and glancing over at his wife to try to read her thoughts, "it's a great honour to be asked I'm sure. I'd rather not turn it down. Ah, yes, I'll accept the offer. I'll be glad to accept if I'm the choice of the Corporation."

"Then the matter's settled," said Parle rising to his feet and shaking Ferguson's hand. "You'll understand that Lambert's funeral is on Saturday, meaning your inauguration will most likely be the following one. You can call to the town hall after market. Out of respect for Lambert's relatives, I'm sure you'll appreciate that the process will be unceremonious this time around. We can convene an extraordinary meeting of the Corporation at five o'clock at which you'll be sworn in."

"Oh, yes, yes," concurred Ferguson. "Let's keep it all as quiet as possible."

"Very well then, consider yourself Mayor-elect. Being Lambert's Deputy I can perform, as Acting-Mayor, such duties as are required of the office for the next nine days. In the meantime, congratulations."

Having shaken Robert's hand once more and also made a show of courtesy to Mrs. Ferguson, Alderman Parle departed the scene. That Lucy Ferguson's husband was gruntled by the glad news of his appointment was obvious. His face beamed and an air of triumphant satisfaction hung all around him just then.

"Well," he said, folding his arms and leaning back against the closed door, "I'm to be Town Mayor. How about that Lucy?"

CHAPTER 16

Echoes from the Past

On the same night that Alderman Parle had called to Slaneyview House and informed its master of his nomination for Mayor, there came a second knock at the door of that grand domicile. Mrs. Lucy Ferguson, expecting that the Deputy Mayor was returning to clarify some minor detail of the arrangements for her husband's accession, opened the door herself this time. Her husband was by now on his way to bed. But the man at the door was not Alderman Parle. It was Jacob.

"Beggin' yer pardon, Mrs. Ferguson," he began doffing his hat to the woman, "but bein' the wife o' the most prominent barley merchant in the barony I was sorta wonderin' if yeh could put in a good word for us to yer husband. It's just that I'm out of a position right now and have a good knowledge o' the grain business."

"It is not a matter with which I am familiar, Jacob. You will need to call to the mill in person on the morrow."

"But Mrs. Ferg—"

"My husband has had a long day and has just retired to bed."

"But Mrs. Ferguson, maam," he protested, "won't yeh put in a word for us? I mean, given that we go back all these years and I was at the camp in Wales when yeh were there an' all."

"I don't recollect you, Jacob," she replied starting to close over the door.

"But I remember *you*, Mrs. Ferguson," he contended. "Won't yeh help me t'earn a few bob?"

By now the door was firmly closed. Jacob left the scene depressed and dejected. He walked solemnly back towards his cottage in the east of the town, cursing the name of Lucy Ferguson more than once on his journey. Meanwhile the woman's spirit was not a little disturbed by his revelation. She genuinely had not remembered his being at the camp in Wales. But then it was a quarter of a century ago and he was unlikely to have learnt anything of her exploits with Michael Hendrick.

Some fifteen minutes or so later, yet a third visitor knocked at the door of the Ferguson residence. The couple were both in the process of retiring for the night and Lucy was already in her nightclothes. She looked at her husband in surprise, saying "three visitors inside an hour?" With a sigh, Robert descended the stairs and answered the door.

"Good night to yeh, sir," said the visitor. "I'll not keep y'up. I'm just here about a little unfinished business."

The man at the door was Hendrick. He informed Ferguson that there were certain items of a sensitive nature that had been stashed under a floorboard in the kitchen. The two men proceeded thither and removed the floorboard in question. Hendrick then lay on the floor. Reaching under and feeling his way around for a few moments, he produced a large bundle of papers that were wrapped in brown paper. By now Lucy was on the landing attempting to overhear any discourse that was likely to take place between the two men. To Ferguson's surprise and agitation Hendrick took the liberty of sitting himself down at the kitchen table and unwrapping the bundle he held.

"Well Ferguson," he began, "yel remember a story I once told of an unhappy predicament I got meself into in Wales? And how the woman in question hounded me for years after?"

"Oh I remember it well. Don't tell me she's still onto you, is she?"

"Well, thankfully no," he replied. "She's after marryin' so she is. As yeh can expect her correspondence to me was halted almost overnight. So I've nottin' to fear from her now. And I've nottin' agin her. But harken to this."

By now Ferguson was physically and mentally exhausted from the rigours of the day, and all he wished for was a sound night's sleep. But he entertained his rival for a time.

"Oh hear me dear Michael," he began reading. "It may be a matter of trivia to you now. But not to me. My devotion to you, ever since that night, cannot be counted. I long to return to you Michael. Surely your wife and daughter are truly lost to you now. You should run the risk of her return, slight as it is, and be wed to me. For my part, I cannot ever truly give my love to another man so long as you are alive and there is a chance of our being re-united. Yes Michael, it's you or nobody for me."

Hendrick proceeded to unfold and to read aloud another half dozen or so of these letters. Ferguson was only mildly interested but was willing to tolerate the wretched man for another few minutes at any rate. As he approached the end of each epistle it sounded to the Mayor-elect that Hendrick would indeed announce the signed name of the woman in question. But it was never his intention so to do.

"Eh, I think you should not perhaps tell me her name, Michael," pleaded Ferguson. "You say that she's now a married woman and maybe the whole matter should be allowed to rest don't you think. If even for the name of her new husband, whomever that may be, if you've no concern left for her own.

"Well, well, I suppose y'are right Ferguson," admitted Hendrick. "It would do an untold injury to them both. Yeh can be sure o' that!"

To Ferguson's lasting relief, Hendrick at length rose from the table and gathered up his bundle of letters once more. As Hendrick's disdain for his former friend was not altogether replicated by that man (at least on anything like the scale) Ferguson made his former friend an offer upon their parting.

"Eh, you'll no doubt be aware Michael," he began, "that there's always an extra pair of hands needed at the mill. I'd just like you to know that you're always welcome. Call in at any time and we'll see you right."

Hendrick was puzzled at Ferguson's motivation for this apparent generosity. Did he feel, in his inmost being, that the extent to which he had supplanted Hendrick in the town was more even than the miserable man deserved? Was it out of mere charity at Hendrick's straightened circumstances? Or was it that the mill was indeed so prosperous as to always require additional labour? For now he did not really care. Stultifying as such labour could often be, Hendrick had no choice but to work for Ferguson. By the time he had arrived at Jacob's cottage he had resolved to call to the mill first thing the following day. This news was, however, not particularly well received by Jacob.

"Well I don't know what y'are bein' so gloomy about Jacob," insisted Hendrick. "Neither of us had the means o' keepin' body and soul together for very long. Now there'll be an income at the cottage as will keep us both."

Jacob was one of those curious individuals that derived a sort of perverse pleasure from revealing to others any news that may seem unwelcome in their ears, particularly when he could pretend that he believed the news was likely already known.

"So yel be workin' for the new Mayor, eh?" he said. "Yeh *have* heard o' Doctor Lambert's demise no doubt? And that yer new employer is to succeed him as Town Mayor."

"Well, I never knew he was goin' to be Town Mayor," replied Hendrick. "It wasn't somethin' he mentioned to me."

"Only heard it meself about twenty minutes ago. Seems poor aul' Lambert passed away in his bed!"

"Ah well," murmured Hendrick resignedly, "what's to be will be. Ferguson as Mayor, eh? Who'd have thought it?"

Some eight months later, the day finally arrived when Hendrick would be released from his twenty-one year vow of abstinence. After initially indulging himself as if to make up for lost time, the man only rarely partook of alcoholic beverages thereafter, doing so in such quantities as to be only 'a little tipple' or 'one for the road'. The fact was that, being a man of seemingly limitless energy, he was making no small impression in his labours at the mill. A combination of this determined industriousness, Hendrick's ready availability for any additional hours that were on offer and the paltry sum that he paid to Jacob every week for his humble lodgings actually resulted in Hendrick's managing to save a little money of his own. As the summer passed and Ferguson began his second term as Mayor, Hendrick was joined at the mill by his stepdaughter.

"Ah, is it here that y'are workin'?" he asked her jovially.

"Yes father," she replied enthusiastically. "Robert says there's always extra hands needed this time of year, what with harvest on the way and all."

In spite of his growing distinctly cold towards the girl having learnt of her true parentage, Hendrick found that she was in fact the only real source of happiness in his life. There could be no resisting the warmth of her daughterly devotion (farcical at it seemed to a mere stepfather) and Hendrick nurtured such an affection for her as if she nearly had been his very own flesh and blood.

By the following spring Hendrick had, through patient industry and meticulous husbandry, managed to save up the princely sum, or so it seemed, of £12. The spark of enterprise, still not completely quenched in the man, was rekindled once more as Hendrick began considering the uses to which his hard-earned resources may profitably be put. On walking to work one morning in early February, Hendrick noticed that a small property near the canal bridge was for sale. It was in fact a structure contiguous to The Pikeman's Inn, and consisted of two downstairs and three upstairs rooms.

"Supposing I was t'open a little shop o' some sort," he murmured to himself. "Nottin' serious just a little store for seeds or fertilisers or somethin' o' the sort. Then I could live in th'upstairs."

The price set on the property was £60 and Hendrick made enquiries forthwith. The following afternoon he arrived at the bank for a meeting with Mr. Sweetman, the very banker who had presided over the repossession of his business and of Slaneyview House a couple of years before. Hendrick was mildly startled to notice that a third party had been invited to the meeting, that of Robert Ferguson the Town Mayor.

"Good day to yeh both," he said taking off his hat and sitting himself down in Sweetman's spacious office.

"Well Mr. Hendrick," began Sweetman leaning forward, "things look even more hopeful for you than you'd expected. If as you say you're planning to open a small outlet of your own on the premises, the Corporation has agreed to award you a new business grant of twelve pounds. In addition, they're offering to lend you a further fifteen pounds at a nominal rate of interest. We at the bank are satisfied that you learnt the lessen of your rashness in that infamous harvest a couple of years back. If you're willing to put up ten pounds of your own money towards the business, the bank will happily lend you the remainder. Now there can't be a fairer deal than that. What do you say, Mr. Hendrick?"

Within minutes a large sign was placed over the premises. It read "**SOLD**". At long last, fortune was beginning to favour Michael Hendrick. On arriving home he informed Jacob that he was grateful for the latter's hospitality but would no longer require lodgings at his cottage. Within days Hendrick was off to his new home to brace himself for a brand new venture. On exiting the cottage for the last time he threw the parcel of letters on the kitchen table and asked Jacob to deliver them to Lucy Ferguson at first light tomorrow.

"Be sure *he's* not at home when yeh visit, Jacob. Take care to give it to his wife in person, won't yeh?"

"If it's yer wish, Michael," replied Jacob.

"Good on yeh. Well, I'm off. Best o' luck to yeh."

CHAPTER 17

❦

Dusty and Krusty

The location of Michael Hendrick's new outlet could not have been more advantageous to its proprietor. Whenever the season for planting arrived, numerous farmers from the county 'round would pass through the centre of Castlebridge on their way to Wexford Town—some hailing from as far away as Monamolin, Ballygarrett and Ballycanew. But now, as they rode down Main Street and passed the turn for Blackwater Road on their left, a brand new and brightly painted shop front greeted them on their right. Its lettering was

"HENDRICK'S FERTILISERS
ESTD. 1837".

In those first few months of trading, Hendrick's venture far exceeded even his own ambitious expectations. The prices he charged for his bags of fertiliser were, given the modest size of the venture, a little higher than those on offer at the major stores in Wexford Town. But the farmers who passed through, cute foxes to a man, well knew that their avoiding the punitive tolls incurred on crossing Wexford Bridge more than compensated for such slight inflations. Thus, Hendrick's business throve.

By now Megan-Leanne had grown weary of Slaneyview House. It had been the home in which her dear mother had passed away and where Hendrick had subsequently staked his claim to the girl's paternity. It had since become the property of the man she loved to distraction but in which her companion and former mistress now lived as that man's wife. For Megan, this domestic arrangement was far from ideal. She had for some time harboured intentions of finding a place to call her own. She did not need to look far. The rooms above the new fertiliser shop, though a good deal smaller than she'd been accustomed to either in Slaneyview House or in Oldtown Manor, were at least comfortable, convenient and functional. Thus, she was warmly admitted by her stepfather.

Jacob, meantime, sat dismally in his bohaun, by now nursing grudges against Hendrick, Ferguson *and* Ferguson's wife. Breaking the confidence of his former tenant, he audaciously proceeded to open the bundle of letters that Hendrick had so negligently charged him with delivering to the Mayor's wife. Yielding to his own vulgar curiosity, he trawled through the bundle of Lucy's correspondences and wondered at the woman's directness. Had Hendrick detected any such a breach of trust there would have been a serious confrontation between the two, one in which Jacob was likely to fare worse than his antagonist. He speedily folded them all and replaced them tidily in their parcel. But it was some weeks before he finally got around to taking the parcel under his arm and proceeding towards the town centre. It was a late afternoon in April when he finally undertook to fulfil his promise. Strolling towards Main Street, the milling complex to his right, Jacob noticed that a shabbily dressed female figure was bending over the lower bridge and appeared to be spitting into the canal. It was none other than Nancy Muckridge. In all her crude rusticity, she'd been attempting to strike the reeds and other canal bank foliage with her projectile spittle. This was one of her own personal favourite pastimes. Nancy was indeed widely considered one of the more benign of her ilk, being as they were no strangers to all manner of vice.

"Oi, Jacob lad!" she bellowed. "Is it up the town y'are goin'?"

"It surely is. Only a little errand I've got Nancy, nottin' urgent."

"I'm thinkin' to meself it's a quare long while since we seen aul' Jacob down at Dusty's and no mistake. Y'aven't been inside the place in a good three months for sure. I, for wan, can't recall sein' yeh fillin' yerself up there this side o' Christmas."

The imbibing emporium to which the unschooled rustic referred was Dusty Doyle's. It was located near to the bottom of a narrow thoroughfare called Dixon Lane. In spite of its renown as a centre of unrivalled economic prosperity, Castlebridge also had its dark side. In spite of its many virtues, Castlebridge had its vices. These were all too obvious if one ventured to journey down Dixon Lane.

Long since knocked down, a narrow laneway there was in the east of the town. This was the Pollregan end of Castlebridge. 'The Lane', as it was called locally, served as home to all that was odious, all that was loathsome, all that was depraved and all that was vile. Hideously begrimed tenements lined either side of Dixon Lane, daily disgorging onto it their several noxious odours, foul diseases and unwholesome utterances. One of the enigmas that always surrounded Dixon Lane was the origin of its name. For at this time, the Dixons were one of the most respected and prosperous of all Castlebridge families. The building of the famous Castlebridge Canal, of which mention has already been made, was masterminded earlier in the century by a genius engineer called Dixon. It was indeed one of the cruellest of ironies that a family reputed for bringing so much unprecedented prosperity to the town shared its name with the location for the most iniquitous and reprobate activities in the neighbourhood. It was impossible for any visitor to Dixon Lane to depart from the place unmoved, and duller shouldst he be than the great bard's fat weed that roots itself in ease on Lethe wharf wouldst he not stir in this. Dixon Lane simply breathed putridity.

The nucleus of daily life in The Lane was its public house, Dusty Doyle's. Any disregard that frequenters of The South Leinster Arms nurtured for patrons of The Pikeman's Inn paled beside the contempt in which both held the regular crew at Dusty Doyle's. If the conduct at The Pikeman's Inn could occasionally be deemed to be somewhat purgatorial, then there could be no doubting that at Dusty Doyle's it was verifiably infernal. One of the most pernicious of its regular patrons was a loud-mouthed, half-shaven, malodorous and depraved old rogue by the name of Krusty. He was in his mid-fifties. His face was rough, his features sharp and he spoke with a harsh, grating voice. Nancy Muckridge cajoled Jacob into partaking of a 'tipple or two' in this notorious establishment and he was received therein almost as though he were the returning prodigal son.

"Oi! Hey! Would yeh be lookin' who's after droppin' in for an aul' mouthful o' stout with us," bellowed Krusty the moment he caught sight of Jacob entering the inn. "I'm cursed if that's not aul' Jacob from the bohaun above."

"It surely is," confirmed Nancy Muckridge. "And it's a whole belly full he's needin' if the truth be told. Look how sad he's lookin', eh? C'mon Doyle, if ever I seen a man with a dry throat it's now."

Jacob's countenance certainly wore a distinctly crestfallen appearance that night. The new master at the mill had neglected to furnish him employment, that man's wife had regarded his appeals with stark disinterest, and his only income source of late—the modest rent paid him by Hendrick—had been discontinued. He sat brooding over his bottle as Muckridge, Krusty and several others of the swinish louts there present tried to elevate him from this current state of despondency. Not being folk of strong imagination, they failed. As he became by stages more and more inebriated, his mood evolved from one of dolefulness to one of ill temper and thence to one of venomous spite. He had completely overlooked his commission from Hendrick. Suddenly amidst all the clamour, Krusty raised a large clumsy hand in the air and, himself the worse for drink, lowered it down pointing in the direction of where Jacob sat.

"Wow now folks. Listen to me!" he shouted. "That fella sittin' there. D'yeh see him? That fella Jacob that aul' Muckridge is after bringin' in here. He looks to be carryin' some class o' pack 'n' fardel under his arm. Suppose he tells us what's in it, eh? Well Jacob lad?"

At this Nancy Muckridge and the others severally stalled in their boisterous chatter to stare at the man. Even Dusty Doyle himself leaned over the counter to see if he could establish what all the clamour was in aid of. Jacob, by now in a state of semi-somnolence, lifted his face from the arm he was resting it on and began to murmur something to the folks gathered round.

"This parcel, folks, ah now, wouldn't yeh just love to know what's inside eh? Well let me tell the lot o' yeh!" he said gradually rousing himself and attempting to sit as straight as was possible in the circumstances. "Inside this pack 'n' fardel, oh yes, this here very parcel that I hold in me hand, is a treasury o' secrets. Oh, yes, yeh better be believin' it. Yel not be creditin' the passion o' some of these, oh no. What's more, will I tell yeh whose name it is that's writ upon them, eh? It's none other than the Town Mayor's wife!"

"Mrs. *Ferguson* yeh mean?" interposed Krusty.

"The very woman, though she was a Devereux in them days y'understand," said Jacob. "There must be a score o' letters in here and it's none other than Lucy that's after signin' every last wan o' them."

"But who in the name o' Gad are they addressed to?" enquired Nancy Muckridge.

"None other," began Jacob slowly unfolding the first of the letters, "than Mr. Michael Hendrick. Here, let me read yiz a few."

"*Hendrick!*" exclaimed Dusty from over the bar. "Can it be that a passion existed between Lucy Ferguson and aul' Hendrick 'pon a time?"

Then an eerie silence fell over the whole public house as Jacob began to read aloud several of the intimate correspondences in his possession. Thus the details of Lucy's past that had remained concealed for so many years were, in an instant, uncovered and publicly promulgated at Dusty Doyle's. As the fifth or sixth of these letters was being read aloud, Krusty started waving his finger in a contemplative manner.

"Yeh know somethin'?" he proclaimed. "I've a way o' gettin' some o' these writin's into The Castle & Bridge. Yel not believe it but it's true as day. I know a fella workin' there who'll do it without protestin' to me."

Krusty was right. For an erstwhile friend had confided in him some years ago when that friend had got into difficulties—difficulties indeed not unlike those of Michael Hendrick's. Krusty was a malicious man and perfectly devoid of sentiment. What's more, he had a heart inaccessible to any compassionate influence. Owing to these facts the friend, who by now enjoyed a position of some seniority at the local newspaper, had left himself helplessly exposed to the rogue's blackmail. Compromised thus, he could not but comply with any request on Krusty's part to publish such communications. Assuring his peers that he could force a member of staff at The Castle & Bridge to publish almost any article he required them to, Krusty advanced to one all important detail; namely the timing of any such publication. Several dates were proposed and all agreed that a week on which there was expected to be a high circulation was certain to have the greatest impact.

"They're bound to be markin' forty year o' the struggle 'pon Vinegar Hill," offered one local rustic, a thin and crumpled man who was easily old enough himself to have fought in it. "Surely it's the wan week yel get every last home i' the town buyin' it!"

"Ah well Cheevers, yeh may be right there," replied Krusty. "But it's over a year away. Just like th'election for Mayor. That's not for a full year ayther."

"I'm thinkin' to meself," said Nancy Muckridge speculatively, "that we might not be needin' to wait long. Now listen to me, the lot o' yeh. It's put about that aul' King Willie ails from a bit o' th'aul' pneumonia. I hear tell abroad that he's not much time left him. So now, if yel wait until he finally drops off, yel have yer audience then, eh?"

"Ah, be off would yeh Muckridge," interjected Cheevers. "Sure what would th'honest folk o' Wexford be doin' to folli the comin's an' goin's yonder? Wasn't it agin the crown we were fightin' in ninety-eight?"

"It surely was, Cheevers," concurred Muckridge. "But yel not credit th'interest in Castlebridge when aul' George went down seven year ago. A fair readin' and no mistake."

After a good deal of debating on the subject, it was finally agreed to await the imminent demise of the ruling monarch and, in the expectation of a higher than average circulation of The Castle & Bridge, to arrange to publish the letters in coincidence of that event.

There was one customer of Dusty Doyle's that night that had hitherto desisted from contributing to the conclave. He appeared to be a visitor to Castlebridge and was seated alone in a corner of the tavern. He was about forty years of age, had striking red hair and a lean, heavily freckled face. From the moment he raised his voice to speak, his accent and the speed at which he spoke told one and all that he was undoubtedly a member of the itinerant community. He was in fact a tin-dealer and the head of a large itinerant family that was passing through Castlebridge on their way to the town of Arklow some nine or ten leagues to the north. The visitor's name was Tim Cash. He had given the impression of one languishing in passive inattention but had an eager ear and had learnt much of his co-patrons' intentions.

"I've overheard what y'are doin' with them love letters 'n' all," he said. "I'm only passin' through town but I can tell y'all that nottin' good will come of it for sure. Bad luck yeh know, to be noisin' such intimate letters as them."

"Ah, what superstitious folk th'aul' tinkers are," exclaimed Krusty. "If yeh knew the woman as well as us, not to mention the fella she's after havin' such a wild passion for, yed not be spoilin' the party, eh?"

With that the visitor rose, gathered up his cap from the table, and spoke gravely.

"It's a curse that'll come of it, be sure. Nottin' but bad luck!"

The tinker then regarded the half-drunken state of each of the patrons gathered round, shook his head admonishingly, and left the shady tavern forthwith.

CHAPTER 18

✸

The Longest Day

Early the next morning (yet late enough for Ferguson to have departed his home for the mill), Jacob finally undertook to deliver his parcel to the Mayor's wife. Without hesitation, Lucy Ferguson destroyed every last particle of evidence of her former encounters with Hendrick. It being now early summer, the lighting of any fire would have aroused her husband's suspicion. So it was that Lucy strolled to the riverbank at the bottom of her long sloping garden. Tossing the now torn letters into the water, she convinced herself that this chapter of her personal history was at last confined to a watery grave.

So the weeks passed and preparations got underway for the town's annual Midsummer Fair. Though always held on the fourth Saturday in June, this year that date would conveniently coincide with Mid-Summer's Day itself—namely June the twenty-fourth. A special Midsummer 'bumper' edition of The Castle & Bridge newspaper was to be printed that week. Given that Midsummer was the only occasion in the entire year that many folks bothered to read that weekly publication, it was arranged in advance to produce double the normal batch in anticipation of such inflated demand.

As Wednesday the twenty-first of June dawned, excitement mounted both within Castlebridge and in the county 'round. The office of The Castle & Bridge was a hive of activity as finishing touches were applied to a publication so eagerly awaited by the townsfolk. Krusty, along with several of his shady accomplices at Dusty Doyle's, had grown weary in a seemingly endless wait for news of the King's demise. And so there was a change of plan. The Editor-in-Chief of The Castle & Bridge was given strict instructions to include in its Midsummer edition many sordid details of the long-passed intimacies between Michael Hendrick and the woman who was now the Mayor's wife.

Suddenly, at about midday, a coach was seen bounding up Ardcavan Road with furious recklessness. It tore into the town leaving a half-blinding dust trail in its wake. Its master drove as though charging an enemy. With a wild rattle and clatter, and an inhuman abandonment of consideration for pedestrians, it dashed across the outer canal bridge and swept up Main Street knocking over not a few minor obstacles in the process. It then came to an abrupt halt outside the offices of The Castle & Bridge, where two men dismounted and ran to the door beating on it loudly.

"Stop Press! Stop Press!" they shouted. "*The King is dead! Stop Press! Stop Press! The King is dead!*"

Whatever the overarching effects of the quest for Irish freedom, culminating as that struggle had done on Vinegar Hill some four decades earlier, the local newspaper's omitting to mention as noteworthy an event as the passing of a monarch would have been editorial and commercial suicide. The newspaper's offices were instantly thrown into frenzied pandemonium. To postpone by a week any coverage of the death would have caused many townsfolk to regard this hitherto esteemed local paper as out of date and irrelevant. It was mandatory that front-page coverage would be allocated to the event. If The Castle & Bridge was to go to press on time, some form of tribute would need to be worded with great haste. And so it was.

Very early the next morning, indeed not long after four o'clock, Ferguson rose and prepared himself for a journey of many leagues. He had a pressing business appointment at Enniscorthy and would need to arrive early were he to secure a lucrative barley deal. He kissed his wife goodbye and drove swiftly away into the still morning. Some hours after Lucy Ferguson heard the sound of her husband's carriage scurrying out of the drive and across Codd's Bridge, she roused herself. Opting to remain in bed for her own ease she called for Hartley to deliver her breakfast thither. It being a Thursday, this would naturally be accompanied by The Castle & Bridge.

"Please ma'am," he said on entering the room. "Your breakfast as requested. It's black coffee and croissants, lightly buttered just as you like them. And this week's newspaper. Plenty of reading today ma'am, what with the fair and all this fuss over the death of King William."

"Indeed Hartley, indeed," she replied. "Very good. I shall take my leisure this morning and should rise at ten today I think. That'll be all."

The Mayor's wife sat up in bed and began to take her breakfast. Allowing the coffee a few moments to cool, she unfolded her newspaper and engrossed herself in its lead page. In most of the colonies, tidings pertaining to the ruling monarch were received with any one of enthusiasm, indifference, distaste or even ridicule. For Lucy Ferguson, they held an almost mesmerising fascination. Royal stories, however trivial or contrived, were compulsive reading for this woman of wealth, property and social stature.

Entirely oblivious to the explosive revelations on its subsequent pages, she fervently scanned the face of her newspaper and became totally immersed in any article that related to the King's death. She read how William was described by some as 'warm-hearted', by others 'eccentric', by others 'unimpressive', and by others still 'lacklustre'. One article named ten children born to the man by an Irish actress with a Wexford surname, an actress he would later disown and abandon upon unexpectedly coming in line to the throne. Another, in seeming contradiction, referred to his 'exemplary private life and disdain for pomp and ceremony'.

Though he was described by some as a weak, ignorant, commonplace sort of person, the general thrust of the editorial was appreciative. It paid tribute to the man's radical parliamentary reforms. It told how his was the only monarchy of the age to survive the advent of democracy, how his unremarkable character was instrumental in his passing through that era unscathed, how not one of his fourteen children could succeed him to the throne (owing either to their dying in infancy or to their non-royal maternity), and how that throne was now occupied by his niece, a young maiden of barely eighteen years. Little mention was made of his having spat publicly on his own coronation day.

Megan-Leanne, meanwhile, was preparing breakfast for herself and her stepfather in their cosy dwelling above the latter's retail outlet. Hendrick, in his eagerness to open the little fertiliser shop at its allotted time, ate his breakfast with some alacrity and left The Castle & Bridge on the breakfast table having only half-interestedly glanced over its cover page. Megan-Leanne, not to be rushed, poured herself more tea and began slowly turning its pages. Having digested the lead story, she continued to search the newspaper's contents for any articles that might be of interest to her. She seemed particularly interested in any feature that related to the upcoming Midsummer Fair, which was now only two days away.

The town bell rang for nine o'clock. Today being the longest day of the year, the sun had already risen to lofty heights. Megan could hear the hustle and bustle on the street below as she continued to absorb that which she was reading. Suddenly her eyes were drawn to a headline that sent a short, sharp, shiver down her spine. Her face lost any colour it had worn and her lips began to quiver violently. Indeed, the poor girl was in such agitation that she could hear her own heart thudding violently. She leaned over the newspaper and read and read and read it over and over and over again. It was not an hallucination. She was no longer in slumber and dreaming strange dreams. This was real. The Castle & Bridge was revealing details of an intimacy it claimed had once taken place between the man she called her father and the Town Mayor's wife. She ran to the window, which was already open given the sultry morning, and threw her head out of it glancing up and down the street. For some minute or two she paced up and down the kitchen in something of a panic, then grabbed the newspaper, raced downstairs to the fertiliser shop, thrust the paper into Hendrick's hands and spoke to him breathlessly.

"Father!" she gasped. "I *must* see Mrs. Ferguson. You've not read The Castle & Bridge. They've printed an awful scandal about you both. They're claiming you and she were lovers once, which is cruel and vicious and surely untrue. You'll need to send for Lawyer Creane. I must hasten to Slaneyview House. It's not yet ten so perhaps she has not had occasion to read it. I must forewarn her. It's best if I go now father."

Before Hendrick could even answer, his stepdaughter had torn out of the shop and onto the street. To the bewilderment of most of the townsfolk, Megan-Leanne could be seen pelting up Main Street as fast as her legs could carry her, then straight along Codd's Walk and up the drive of Slaneyview House. She thumped on the door violently. Presently Hartley answered the knock but by now Megan was helplessly out of breath.

"What's the matter?" the butler enquired concernedly. "What ails yeh?"

"Hartley," she wheezed, "I must see your mistress! You have to let me see her!"

"But Mrs. Ferguson is not disposed to see anyone just now. I've not yet been to her room to collect her breakfast things and *Mr.* Ferguson is on an important business errand to Ennisco—"

"*Hore!*" she interrupted barging her way into the hall at site of the household's chambermaid. "Will *you* let me speak to Mrs. Ferguson? Tell her it's urgent. Hartley says she's still in bed. I must speak to the lady soon!"

"Still in bed?" repeated the chambermaid. "Mistress is not in bed. I've just been to the linen room and I seen her on the landing, dressed an' all. She seemed fierce anxious about somethin' though. So I says to her what's wrong and can we help? Mrs. Ferguson shakes her head at me, says she's in need of a little fresh air, and says she'll just take a little turn around the garden for a while. Nice summer mornin' that it is I thought nottin' of it and let her be. I'm sure Mrs. Ferg—"

There was little point in continuing. Megan was down the hallway in a flash. With consummate velocity she ripped through the kitchen knocking down several utensils, which clanged and clattered to the floor in her wake. She raced into the sloped back garden and feverishly searched for her companion. Hartley and Hore, meanwhile, remained in the hallway in stupefaction.

Several seconds later they heard a loud ferocious scream from the bottom of the garden. The two servants glared at each other for a moment, and then with one accord hurried to the back garden. All that could be seen at the bottom of the garden was the crumpled figure of Megan-Leanne. She was kneeling by the riverbank and sobbed bitterly with her head bowed low to the grass. As the butler and the chambermaid approached, the horror of the scene became instantly apparent to both. There, in the stream that ran out from under Codd's Bridge and formed the boundary of the Ferguson estate, was a body lying face down and motionless on the surface. It was the drowned remains of Mrs. Lucy Ferguson. Megan was convulsed with grief and the two servants stood over her, aghast at the sight.

"What about her husband?" cried Megan looking up, her eyes still streaked with tears. She seized the chambermaid with both hands. "He must be told about this at once!"

"Mr. Ferguson's at Enniscorthy miss," replied Hore. "He rose early this mornin' and is not due back before tea."

By now a crowd had begun to gather at Codd's Bridge and Constable Burke had hurried to the scene. Then an idea struck Megan. She tore out of the garden and, with the urgency of Lot fleeing Sodom, raced back towards her stepfather's fertiliser shop. When she arrived she noticed that Fogarty the local candlestick-maker had called into the shop for a chat with Hendrick. Hendrick appeared severely perturbed by the newspaper's revelations but his heart sank yet further when Megan burst onto the scene and related to him the sorry news of Lucy Ferguson's suicide.

"Father!" she gasped, the tears streaming down her cheeks. "It's the most tragic of scenes. I found her floating there in the stream. How horrifying! What could have possessed her? Was it all really that bad? What about Robert? They tell me he's away at Enniscorthy to visit some barley dealer or something. Oh, won't somebody send for him and bring him back? His poor wife is drowned and he knows nothing of it."

"*Fogarty*," cried Hendrick, "can't yeh look after the shop for us a couple o' hours? We got to get hold of a chaise and track down Ferguson. We'll not be long. He should be headin' back at about midday so chances are we'll meet him upon the road."

"Yeh might do Hendrick," replied Fogarty. "But he's a call at Oylegate after lunch and another at Ballimurn I'm told. It's wan o' them two yeh should be headin' for."

"We'll do just that but we best be off now. Will yeh keep the shop for us?"

"I surely will. And my advice, for what it's worth, it to take the Crossabeg Road to Kyle Cross and just head northward on th'Enniscorthy Road. It's Oylegate he'll be visitin' first so I'd get yerselves there before him."

As planned, a chaise was hastily procured. Hendrick and his stepdaughter then headed with all manner of speed up Main Street and along Codd's Walk. They did halt temporarily on Codd's Bridge but only to inform Constable Burke of their intentions. Burke approved but further requested that Megan call to the police station some time later, she being the first to discover the dead body. The horse neighed violently and rose to his hind legs. Then tearing across the bridge and up the Crossabeg Road, the party drove out of the town and into the country.

Some time later they were on the southern outskirts of the quaint village of Oylegate. Hendrick slowed the chaise and immediately scanned the locality for evidence of anyone familiar. Having once been the most important barley dealer in the area, he did not have a long wait. There at the side of the road stood a small stocky man with a round, rugged face and huge sideburns. Hendrick recognised him instantly as Farmer Doran of Edermine.

"Oi! Dor'n!" he exclaimed stepping down from the carriage.

"Is it yerself Hendrick?" replied the farmer amicably.

"Dor'n," continued Hendrick with some urgency. "Are y'expectin' Robert Ferguson to be here today? Or do yeh know who he's supposed to be meetin' in this place?"

"Well we're not expectin' him *back*, if that's what yeh mean," responded Doran. "He was here only about fifteen minute ago. Says he's off to Ballimurn to collect some barleycorn at a farmyard."

"*Whose* farm, Dor'n? Can yeh tell us whose farm he's headin' to?"

"I surely can. It's the farm of aul' Terry and Betty Stamp, just outside o' Ballimurn. That's where he's headed."

"Good on yeh, Dor'n. Then that's where we're headed too."

With that Hendrick leaped back up into the carriage where he had been eagerly awaited by his stepdaughter. Megan-Leanne having overheard the conversation with Farmer Doran in its entirety, no explanation was needed and the carriage pelted off in the direction of Ballymurn. Within a matter of minutes, Hendrick's carriage halted at the entrance to a large farm on the outskirts of that village. In front of them was another carriage, one that bore the inscription

"Ferguson—Miller, Merchant and Barley Dealer".

What surprised Hendrick, however, was the fact that the barleycorn was being loaded not by Ferguson himself but by none other than Amos Wickham.

"Wickham!" cried Hendrick climbing down from the carriage, "where's yer master? The carriage is here, the barleycorn an' all. What about Ferguson?"

"He's in th'other carriage, sir," replied Wickham. "Yeh see sir, I come up here a little while ago and I'm told to send Mr. Ferguson back to the town as soon as can be. It seems that *Mrs.* Ferguson got into some class of accident or somethin'. Me bein' a common workman, they don't tell me nottin'. But I send him back to the town and he takes the faster carriage, tells me to take the big wan and collect all the greeyan. I didn't think of askin' him any questions sir. I just have to do as he says y'understand."

"Wickham," said his former master, this time with less urgency in his voice. "Yer master's wife is drowned."

"*Drowned!*" gasped Wickham with wide-eyed astonishment. "How did she come drowned?"

"We don't know that lad. It's just best he gets back and finds out as soon as he can."

Wickham stared at the big man for a few moments. "Drowned, drowned," the lad repeated to himself over and over again.

CHAPTER 19

❧

A Knock at the Door

For several weeks the drowning of Lucy Ferguson was the talk of the town. Little else was discussed at The Pikeman's Inn, The Miller's Rest, The South Leinster Arms and even at Dusty Doyle's that summer. Then just as the town was beginning to come to terms with that most tragic and unexpected of events, a second suicide was reported in The Castle & Bridge. It was that of Jacob who, filled with remorse for his revelation at Dusty Doyle's and the irreparable damage it had caused, had in desperation flung himself off Wexford Bridge.

Some weeks later, autumn began to set in and Castlebridge tried to put behind it a most lamentable of summers. On a cool yet pleasantly sunny Friday morning in early October, Hendrick was sitting pensively in his little fertiliser shop when a coach rattled into town and pulled up outside. A large and well-built man dismounted. He knocked at the door of the shop, causing Hendrick to raise his glance (for most folks would simply barge in and wish him a 'good mornin'' before he knew it). This customer was most assuredly a stranger to Castlebridge. Like Hendrick he was majestically tall, but unlike him his large, round face looked weather-beaten and wore a jovial and vivacious expression. He had about fifty winters behind him. Though he gave the impression of one well travelled he had not the grim and stony maturity of his interlocutor. It was this man's accent, however, that most emphatically confirmed his not being from the locality. For he spoke with a sort of 'transatlantic twang' that could not have been acquired on Irish soil. Whatever his origins, that he had spent much of his life in one of the far flung colonies there could be little doubt.

"Well sir," he began in clear, confident tones, "this *is* Hendrick's Fertilisers is it not? Do I have the pleasure of addressing Mr. Hendrick, by any chance?"

"Yeh surely do," replied Hendrick.

The man immediately reached forward and shook the merchant's hand. His grasp, though gentle, was not to be resisted. The texture of his large, muscular, ruddy hand was rough and clasped Hendrick's firmly.

"I don't suppose, sir, that you remember me?"

"Can't say I do," answered Hendrick, shaking his head.

"Well, not to worry too much about that," said the man releasing Hendrick's hand, "because *I* remember *you*, oh yes indeed, yes sirree, *I* remember *you* alright."

Hendrick stared at the man for several moments. He had transacted so much business with so many people over such vast stretches of time that it was difficult to place this strange visitor. Though he had rarely, if ever, had occasion to conduct business with an American the sight of this man stirred something in the deepest recesses of Hendrick's memory. Yet he still could not place him.

"Well even if you'll not remember the face, Mr. Hendrick, I'm sure you'll remember the name. It's Redmond."

"Redmond?" laughed Hendrick. "Then y'are in the right part o' the world. I detect from yer accent, sir, that y'are not from 'round here. My guess is that y'are tracin' yer Wexford roots. Ah, yes, them Redmonds are ten-a-penny in these parts. Now if yeh take th'Ardcavan Road about three mile south yel come to a bridge over the Slaney estuary. Drop into the County Office in Wexford Tow—"

Hendrick stopped abruptly. A shiver went down his spine and all the colour drained from his face. He remained doggedly silent. To the merchant's utter astonishment the man before him was none other than Nicolas Redmond, the mariner to whom he had sold his wife and child some twenty-three years earlier. Hendrick was visibly dumbfounded and stood, mouth open, staring at his visitor as though the latter were a spirit returned from the grave to haunt him.

"It's *you* isn't it?" he gasped after a long pause. "The very sailor who was at Wellingtonbridge that night, twenty-three year ago at this stage, but I thought yeh were dead! I mean, I heard some tale of a collision hundreds o' miles from land somewhere in the North Atlantic. How is it y'are alive? And y'are here in Castlebridge and all?"

"Ah, I suppose you *would* have heard that story, my lad," replied the genial sailor. "Well, there is a grain of truth in it, you know. Oh yes indeed. There *was* a collision involving ourselves and another Canadian vessel. I'm sure Susanna told you that we lived at Rivière-du-Loup just then. Well somehow word got back to the town that I had been drowned. What in fact had happened was that we'd been sailing too fast for such a calm night. For you see, sir, when the weather's calm nobody can spot the breaking waves against the icebergs. When the two ships caught sight of each other each altered their course to avoid a head-on collision, only for the two vessels to career sidelong into two separate icebergs. The hulls of both were ripped asunder by the sharp ice and, from that moment, each was destined to founder. It took some hour or so for the ships themselves to go under. Sadly, many of our men and theirs froze to death in the water. With the help of God, myself and a few others managed to stay alive and scramble onto one of the icebergs. There was myself, our second mate and the ship's cook. By about four o'clock in the morning, a Danish merchant vessel came in sight and rescued us."

"But," interjected Hendrick, "two things still confuse me. For wan, yed have got back to that town with the weird French name, Rivière-sur-la-Mer or whatever it's called, and teamed up with Susanna. And I was told that yer collision happened in the month of August! Where did all them icebergs come from in the middle o' summer?"

The sailor laughed heartily, leaning back and staring up at the ceiling as if the laugh did indeed require the expending of some considerable energy. "I can tell you're not a man of the *sea*."

"Not at all," replied Hendrick. "Always keep both feet on firm ground me. It's from the soil I make me livin' Redmond."

"Well, it's like this," resumed the sailor. "In the late spring when temperatures rise, enormous belts of arctic ice slowly begin to thaw. Pack ice, field-ice and large threatening icebergs all break loose and perilously begin to drift south. What's more, early and late summer can be a mighty dangerous time in those parts without the cover of the round the clock daylight we enjoy in June."

Hendrick may have been something of a world authority on barley, milling or corn dealing, but he was forced to bow to this man's vastly superior knowledge of all matters maritime.

"And now I'll answer your other question," he continued. "The Danish vessel that so mercifully found us was destined for Greenland, having in fact sailed from Canada that night. The vessel being by now farther from its port of departure than its destination, its captain elected to take us ashore in Greenland. And so we landed at the strangest of villages. The Danish crew called the place Gronnedal, though they warned us that the locals knew it only as Kangilinnguit. The place could have been called The Gates of Hades for all we cared. It was land and we'd been saved. Coming ashore we were struck by the extreme remoteness of the place. As not a sinner spoke English, our Danish friends taught us a few useful phrases from *their* tongue. But it seemed that many of the townsfolk couldn't even understand us then. The talked in some strange, drawn-out type of language that none of us could make head nor tail of. Anyway it was some weeks before I returned to Canada, doing so only to discover that Susanna had departed and left word that she wished to settle in Wexford. I let the matter be, Michael, for *you* were her rightful husband."

"That's big of yeh, Redmond," said Hendrick. "Very big of yeh, for Susanna tracked me down and we married again, or let on to marry. That was a good five year ago now."

"I'm glad of it, Hendrick, very glad of it. Well, over in Canada I caught wind that Susanna had died. So I resolved to return to Wexford. I'm aware that she's dead some four years at this stage. No, my good man, I'm not here on Susanna's account nor to trace my family roots in the county. I'm here for my young maiden, Miss Megan-Leanne."

Hendrick was thunderstruck. That same young maiden, though not his blood daughter, was by this time his only source of affection in life. Without her, his very existence would be empty. Were the sailor to reveal all, Megan would revile her stepfather for the years of deception and would most probably depart his presence for good. Hendrick, in such a state, would continue to eek out a living from the fertiliser shop but his life would be directionless, purposeless and void. He would surely die a lonely, unloved and bitter old man. Not in his wildest speculations had he ever conceived the possibility of the sailor's being alive, let alone predicted his sudden and unsolicited arrival at Castlebridge. Hendrick convinced himself that desperate circumstances demanded desperate measures. Thus, he greatly deceived his visitor.

"Megan?" replied Hendrick. "Oh, yes, well she's *your* daughter after all and not *mine*. That's why I'm so surprised y'are here in Castlebridge. For when Susanna died, a good four year ago as you say, Megan believed there was nottin' left for her in these parts. Bein' her stepfather, she and I were never especially close y'understand. With her mother gone, she determined to repair to Canada and to settle there."

"To *Canada*?" gasped the sailor, startled and bewildered. "Back to *Canada*? I'd never have thought of it. But hasn't she left a forwarding address? I mean, don't you and her write, and she must have made some buddies in Castlebridge?"

"She surely has," answered Hendrick, scarcely believing his own audacity. "She returned to that coastal town where y'all lived for a few years. But she told me she'd move around, find a place of her own and then write back to me when she'd settled. But here, my advice is this. Yerself and herself are both well known in that little town so I'm sure if yeh return there and make enquiry 'round the neighbourhood yel track her down in time."

"Oh, well, Rivière is not Castlebridge you know," replied the sailor contemplatively, his deep-set eyes all the while bent upon the floor. "But then you're right. My entire journey's in vain I suppose. A thousand leagues for nothing. That's just the hand that fortune's seen fit to deal me. Ah well, I've no choice but to return. I'll not trouble you again, Mr. Hendrick. Another voyage beckons. I wish you well sir."

Following his valediction the sailor took the merchant's hand once more and shook it, this time slowly and less enthusiastically than before. Then he turned, strolled solemnly towards the door, exited the shop, flagged down the nearest chaise and sombrely headed away in the direction of Wexford Town.

CHAPTER 20

❊

The Sand Dunes of Curracloe

Hendrick had lit a fuse for himself. In sending Nicky Redmond a thousand leagues across the ocean to Canada, the merchant had merely bought himself time. He was all too conscious of the fact that his misdirecting the gullible sailor by sending him away under such false pretences would only serve to delay the inevitable. It was a stay of execution, no more.

Just then a wild fantasy flashed through the merchant's mind. Perhaps, having searched Rivière-du-Loup in vain for his daughter, Redmond would forsake the chase altogether. The transatlantic journey was, after all, a long and cumbersome one. But this notion was short lived. There was more chance of Queen Marie Antoinette having her head sewn back on, and well Hendrick knew it. Whether the sailor would return in five weeks or in five years, Hendrick could scarcely predict. But he unreservedly convinced himself that Redmond must return, openly declaring himself to Megan-Leanne and uncovering the several deceptions under which they had both laboured at the former Mayor's instigation.

Hendrick prayed earnestly that night. He gave thanks that Megan-Leanne was, mercifully, out of town for the morning. As it happened she'd been strolling on Curracloe Beach. He fervently hoped that no chance meeting would reveal all to Redmond on his outward course through Wexford Town. In fact, Hendrick speculated intensely on the timing of the sailor's manoeuvres. He figured that, as Redmond proceeded westward away from Wexford Town, the chances of such a catastrophic revelation lessened almost by the mile. This was particularly relevant as the sailor passed further and further away from the vicinity of Taghmon, the very village where Megan had been born some twenty-two years earlier. He figured that the sailor would likely resolve to lose no time in returning to Canada. As Redmond's departure from Castlebridge had taken place some two hours before midday it was conceivable that his chaise could be driven all the way to New Ross before sunset, where the sailor would likely take lodgings for the night. The next day he would hasten across County Waterford. By early the next week he'd be some forty leagues away at Queenstown in County Cork, whence he would depart on his long and arduous voyage to Canada. But a seed of uncertainty had been planted (and had taken root) in Hendrick's troubled mind.

Meanwhile some three miles down the road, Redmond's chaise was crossing the toll bridge that spanned the Slaney estuary. Wexford Town now lay before him, quaint and picturesque as it basked in the yellow October sunshine. The sailor was crestfallen, having travelled so far for so little. Though Nicky Redmond was a simple man and naïve, he was mildly puzzled by Hendrick's apparent struggle to remember the precise name of the Canadian town to which his stepdaughter had supposedly returned. At one point in the conversation Hendrick had incorrectly named it 'Rivière-sur-la-Mer', another time referring to it in as vague terms as 'that coastal town where y'all lived'.

But the sailor then resignedly convinced himself that Hendrick was not great with Megan-Leanne and the two were less close than they might have otherwise been were Hendrick her actual father. Believing that this would wholly account for Hendrick's seeming disinterest in the girl, Redmond thought nothing more of the matter and drove towards The Port of Queenstown with all manner of haste.

Some five or six hours later, Megan-Leanne burst into her stepfather's shop beaming from ear to ear. Having lead a life hitherto touched by not a few tragedies, and being no stranger to disappointments, such jovial expressions as Megan wore today seemed strangely uncharacteristic of the girl. Furthermore her natural good looks, which held a magnetism for the opposite sex even in her times of grave humourlessness, now illuminated her fair countenance beyond description. If young bachelors of the barony typically regarded Megan-Leanne as 'desirable', she was at such rare times as this irresistibly captivating. Not a few of the townsfolk noted her high spirits that afternoon. She strolled confidently and ebulliently around Castlebridge. Her almost frenzied exuberance evidenced some happy turn of events in the young woman's life.

"*Father!*" she cried grasping Hendrick by the wrists and holding him fast, "something wonderful has happened!"

Her stepfather made no reply but tried to consider what event could possibly have brought so much glee to the girl's face. For a few brief moments Hendrick feared the worst; hers and Nicky Redmond's paths had somehow crossed, the sailor had presented himself to her and yet had forestalled on revealing himself as her true father. But he soon dismissed this probability, for had such an unfortunate coincidence occurred Megan would have most likely returned to Castlebridge accompanied by the sailor himself. Hendrick's treachery would have been laid bare within minutes.

"Dear, dear father," Megan continued, her eyes bright with exultation. "You'll not believe my good fortune. And I know you'll be happy for me, happy as a father can be. Because you've told me so already."

"I *have*?" questioned Hendrick, still bemused at what good fortune could have been bestowed upon his stepdaughter to account for such elated spirits. "What are yeh talkin' about, Megan? Yeh say y'ave good news for me. Well, out with it."

"I love to stroll on Curracloe Beach as you know."

"Yeh surely do. I figured that's where yed been alright."

"Well, I was speaking to Mr. Ferguson last Sunday," she continued, with sprightly cheerfulness, "and he asked if I wished to stroll there again this week. Perhaps I was free on Friday morning and we could stroll together for a time. I enquired if he'd not be at the mill all day Friday and perhaps Sunday would be more convenient. He told me that Mr. Lowney could take care of the mill for a few hours and that Friday afforded more privacy. So I figured he must have something to tell me, matters of a private nature most likely. But he had nothing to *tell* me father. No. Robert had something to *ask* me."

Just then Megan-Leanne raised her stepfather's right wrist up to his face, thereby placing her own left hand in full view of it. There on her third finger shone a beautiful gold ring adorned by a brilliantly glistening diamond. Megan-Leanne was engaged to be married to Robert Ferguson.

Had he not been so arduous in his earlier representations to his stepdaughter, those made while she was domiciled at Oldtown Manor, the merchant may have left himself scope for a qualified disapproval of this union; or at the very least the option of cautioning the young maiden against an early and hasty acceptance of the Mayor's proposal. But how farcical would that seem. He had openly named Ferguson as his own preferred choice of husband for Megan, and from this position there could be no opportune recoiling now that Lucy was gone to her reward. Thus Hendrick received the tidings with an air of feigned satisfaction, disheartening as the circumstance was. As jealousy, anguish, sorrow and a multitude of other emotions pervaded him, his eyes welled with tears—a sight that was not a little discomforting to his stepdaughter.

"Oh, father, I know it's what you have always wanted for me but please don't cry. Yet I know they are tears of joy. And I know you'll be proud to give me away to the Mayor, especially now that he has been left in affluent circumstances."

"Oh I'm truly happy for yeh both," lied Hendrick, restraining himself. Then he enquired of the girl the precise location where her engagement ring had been procured. "But there's no such trade in Castlebridge. I'm certain o' that. If there's wan shop this place doesn't boast then for sure it's a jewellers."

"Of course," concurred Megan-Leanne. "We chose the ring at Banville's, then took lunch at Aspel's Hotel as a sort of celebra—"

"*Banville's o' Wexford Town?*" interrupted Hendrick.

"Naturally. Do you know of any other Banville's jewellery shop in the district?" she enquired with some curiosity at his inquisitiveness.

"No, no, it's just that," Hendrick paused, eying the girl with an expression of grave solemnity. "What time was it that yeh were in the town, Megan?"

"Before lunch of course," she returned, agitated at this line of questioning. "Did I not mention that we lunched at Aspel's Hotel? Well, we'd strolled on Curracloe in the morning. When we were there, Robert led me to one of the higher sand dunes from where we could see the entire beach. I do love to see the coastline, to hear the waves crashing in and to take in the cool sea breeze. Perhaps it's because I was raised in ports and because he, Mr. Redmond, was a mariner and forever telling me tales of the sea."

More than ever Hendrick resented Megan's referring to her real father, and invariably struggled to veil his discomfort on such occasions. They both knew, of course, that Megan-Leanne had lived almost all of her childhood by the sea. But Hendrick, unlike the deceived young maiden, was also acutely conscious of the fact that a sailor's blood coursed through the young woman's veins. Her affinity with environs maritime was wholly accounted for.

"It was the most romantic of scenes," she continued. "After Robert had proposed, doing so on bended knee as is proper, my most urgent wish was to hasten back to Castlebridge to break the happy news to you, my father. As it happened, Robert had already arranged a carriage to take us to Wexford Town. We crossed the bridge and entered Banville's little jewellery shop at about eleven o'clock. Then, having chosen the ring, we dined at Aspel's as I've told you."

The reason that Hendrick was so eager to learn of the precise timing of these coming and goings will be obvious. Redmond had crossed the toll bridge shortly after *ten* o'clock. The merchant speculated that this was about the same time that Ferguson had made his proposal on Curracloe Beach. If so, and assuming the sailor had stalled in Wexford Town for some thirty or forty minutes in preparation for his onward journey, then a catastrophic chance meeting between them would seem to have been avoided by a matter of mere minutes. Indeed, it seemed likely that Redmond was departing the west side of Wexford Town at precisely the same moment that the happy couple were crossing the toll bridge on the east side. But providence, good fortune, divine intervention—who could tell which—had ordered events in such wise that no encounter should take place between them in that particular town and on that particular day.

At the hour for closing the fertiliser shop, it was with a curious combination of relief and jaded solemnity that Hendrick sat himself down in his upper chambers. In his speculative repose, the former Mayor's eyes were subconsciously directed towards the Scripture verse printed for that particular Friday in October. Though Ferguson knew Hendrick to be not a particularly religious man, he'd kept up the Christmas tradition of sending his rival a small gift—namely the perennial Scripture-calendar of which mention has already been made. Today's words read

> "*I returned, and saw under the sun,*
> *that the race is not to the swift,*
> *nor the battle to the strong,*
> *neither yet bread to the wise,*
> *nor riches to men of understanding,*
> *nor yet favour to men of skill;*
> *but time and chance happeneth to them all.*"

The applicability of such philosophical pronouncements to his own circumstances was not a mentally taxing exercise. For Michael Hendrick was no exception to the universal truth that one's values derive in part from one's own predispositions, in part from one's life experiences, and in part from one's choices—the third being often qualified, modified or seasoned by the second. As Hendrick's life evolved—each new reverse teaching him wisdom, each new blessing gratitude—he became by stages more and more fatalistic in his mindset.

Castlebridge enjoyed the reputation for the highest proportion of physically attractive young women in County Wexford, and Robert Ferguson had just paraded *its* prize jewel into Wexford Town as his own fiancée. By an incredible stroke of luck these representations seemed to have escaped the attention of one Nicky Redmond, doing so by an exceptionally narrow margin. Had Hendrick forestalled the sailor's departure from Castlebridge just a few more minutes, then all would be up. Hendrick would now be suffering his stepdaughter's harsh reprisals instead of enjoying her simple and devoted affection. The former Mayor was safe, at least for the present.

In contrast to the morbid tidings it had had occasion to report in the summer, The Castle & Bridge now printed the happy news of the engagement of Megan-Leanne Hendrick to the Town Mayor, Mr. Robert Ferguson. The happy couple were in high spirits that Christmas and their neighbours shared their joy. New Year's Eve was the appointed date for the engagement's official celebrations, and this was also to be the occasion for the formal announcement of the wedding date itself.

Hendrick, meanwhile, considered the whole business with no small sense of dread. Ferguson shared his fiancée's delusion that she was the twenty-four year-old daughter of his former business rival, rather than the twenty-two year-old daughter of Nicky Redmond. Megan's Baptismal Certificate would soon be required of Hendrick, and there could be no question of his producing anything other than the older—incorrect—document. Yet in doing so the former Mayor would light yet another fuse for himself. The inevitability of Redmond's return to Castlebridge niggled and gnawed at Hendrick twenty-four hours a day and seven days a week. It was unlikely that the sailor would return during the inclement depths of winter, yet his re-appearing in the spring seemed a distinct possibility. Were he to return before the wedding this proud seaman would openly declare himself to his daughter, demand that the second—correct—Baptismal Certificate be presented and snatch from Hendrick the one remaining source of joy and comfort in his broken life.

Yet should the mariner return to Castlebridge and present himself *after* the wedding had taken place, the consequences would be too horrific for Hendrick to contemplate. And well he knew it. In addition to the incalculable emotional turbulence such a return was to cause at any time, Redmond's return *after* the marriage would unquestionably propel his daughter into an uncontrollable rage. If there was one thing more than any other that characterised Megan-Leanne Redmond it was her steadfast adherence to principle. The notion that, owing to some bureaucratic anachronism, her marriage to Ferguson was somehow legally invalid, null and void as it were, would irreparably devastate the girl. In fact it would be added to the stark reality that she herself was the product of an adulterous alliance.

This was early Victorian rural Ireland. It was an age when notions of falling in love, life-long commitments made in private—and all other such bilateral arrangements between consenting adults—paled into insignificance compared to the legally binding Contract of Marriage. What was originally ordained as a symbol of love's natural course had become a substitute for it. The institution itself was to be revered and worshipped, taking precedence over that to which it was intended to give expression. What's more there was at that time a misguided doctrine propagated by the self-appointed moral guardians of the nation's conscience. It warned that eternal hellfire and brimstone awaited those audacious enough to physically gratify their beloved without the express and prior sanction of a body external to the union, namely The Church itself. Such dogma was sold on both sides of the religious divide and, in the main, the people bought it. Yet given the bizarre and irregular circumstances surrounding her own upbringing, our heroine could be forgiven for insisting on all manner of propriety.

Musing on his fate and on the disappointments of life, Hendrick finally resolved to take the only honourable course open to him. He must leave Castlebridge. Being well used to companionship with his own thoughts, he would grow accustomed to depending entirely upon his own self-solicitude. Furthermore he must depart the neighbourhood without any intentions of ever returning. The disquietude of his soul did not permit it.

CHAPTER 21

❀

The Departure of Michael Hendrick

Christmas had passed and the New Year was well underway when the dejected merchant finally set a date for his departure from Castlebridge. Mendaciously adding one more deception to the many he had hitherto contrived for the innocent Megan-Leanne, he pretended to his naïve stepdaughter that he had important business to conduct at Enniscorthy, as well as at Gorey—a town far in the north of the county. These consequential dealings would take some days to complete, and it would be necessary for the former Mayor to make a stay of several days away from Castlebridge. His stepdaughter was given charge, temporary as it seemed, of the fertiliser shop.

The first Saturday in March was to be Michael Hendrick's last ever in Castlebridge. He toyed with the idea of a token appearance at his stepdaughter's wedding, but soon dismissed the notion as apt to engender dissatisfaction. Whether it was his own sin of hubris or the uncontrollable forces of fate, Hendrick had lost his wealth, his social position, and his chances at being loved. Nothing could abate the wild waters of his soul. He considered all that had befallen him in the preceding twenty-four years and, though not particularly sentimental by nature, now shed a tear or two. The following afternoon, Megan and the Mayor were engaged in their customary Sunday afternoon stroll on Curracloe Beach. So Hendrick finally put pen to paper and drafted a long letter to his stepdaughter.

Dear Megan,

For the sake of us both and for the sake of your future husband, I have had to make a decision that was both painful and necessary. Megan my dear, I shall not be returning to Castlebridge. Not this week, nor ever. Expect this correspondence to you to be my last. When you have read it in full, you will understand.

I have deceived you for too long. Every year that passed and each new twist of fate in the town has forced me to add one deception to another. Now I must bring the matter, for good or ill, to a conclusion. There's no easy way to impart this news. Megan, Nicky Redmond is your real father. When you arrived in Castlebridge six years ago, I was the more deceived in perceiving you to be the daughter I had sold to the sailor at Wellingtonbridge. Your mother, God rest her saintly soul, did nothing to contradict my assumption during those days. Yet some twenty-four hours after I'd declared myself to be your true father, yes that very weekend, I uncovered a document unambiguously proving that you—Megan-Leanne Redmond—are the only daughter of a sailor named Nicolas Redmond. I enclose the document as proof. The matter is not beyond reasonable doubt, Megan. It is beyond <u>all</u> doubt. The first Megan-Leanne—my Megan-Leanne—was tragically drowned at Dungarvan in her infancy. To substantiate this claim, I also enclose my daughter's memorial card.

None of us can fathom the purposes of the Good Lord, but by the strangest of coincidences your own birth happened to take place on the same day of the year as my Megan's—3rd September—and even occurred at the same time of day. The deed poll I so cajolingly talked you into signing has long since been reduced to ashes. Redmond always was (and continues to be) your correct surname. What's more I'll not add the sin of omission to my countless other transgressions in this matter. Megan, your father is still alive! It will astound you to learn that he came to Castlebridge last harvest, doing so on your account. In fact, the mariner was standing in our shop on the exact same morning that Ferguson made his proposal of marriage to you on Curracloe Beach. I deliberately and unscrupulously lied to your father, informing him that you had chosen to settle in Canada after your mother's death. What a litany of untruths I've weaved to serve my own jealous and self-centred purposes. Please forgive a pitiful and wretched man if you can find it in your heart to do so.

Your father's return to Castlebridge is inevitable, if not imminent. Whether you choose to postpone your wedding on his account is entirely a matter for you and the Mayor. Of one thing you can be certain however, namely that I will not impose myself upon you again. Furthermore, I recently met with Lawyer Creane. Upon your marrying the Mayor, the fertiliser shop is to be sold up and you are to receive a moiety of the sale price. The amount itself, some £30 or so, may seem little to one marrying into great wealth. Yet I offer it as a meagre token of reconciliation for the many wrongs I have perpetrated upon an innocent and devoted young maiden.

Finally Megan, please do not search for me at Enniscorthy or at Gorey. It was never my intention to set up home in either town. Wishing to settle as far away from Castlebridge as is possible, yet without leaving the county I love, I've opted to live out what years are left to me in Newtownbarry. It's on the boundary with County Carlow and some ten leagues up country from Castlebridge. Charitably accompanied by young Amos Wickham, another person whom I have ill-treated in the past, I've opted for a new life as a general labourer. It's quite a busy town and we'll both have the means to keep body and soul together for a time, God willing.

In the meantime pray for a miserable, ungrateful and lonely old rogue such as I.

Yours,

Mr. Michael Hendrick.

Hendrick folded the letter and, almost as soon as the ink was drying upon its superscription, was in a carriage tearing across Codd's Bridge and into the countryside. Though it cost him a hard pang to leave his stepdaughter, he knew that he must live in perpetual exile from Castlebridge.

Megan-Leanne, after having read the letter, was dumbfounded. She'd spent a mere twenty-two years in the world yet was no stranger to all manner of emotional turmoil. She hoped that, with the departure of Mr. Hendrick, her life would finally settle into something more serene and less eventful. When some two or three weeks later she picked up a copy of The Castle & Bridge, she learnt that this was, sadly, not to be. A violent storm had occurred some hundred miles off the coast of Iceland. There, a vessel en route from Canada to Queenstown, ultimately bound for Southampton, had been utterly devastated. Few survived the tragedy. What's more the captain of the vessel—one Nicolas Redmond, a native of Wexford—had gone down with his ship.

All through that spring, Megan-Leanne conjectured on what might have been. There could be no question that her father was destined for Ireland on her account. But it was not to be. Despite her not being a blood relation of

Michael Hendrick, the girl now displayed something of her stepfather's fatalistic outlook on life. She convinced herself that, for whatever reason, her father and she were not to be re-united this side of eternity.

The summer saw Robert Ferguson begin his third and final term as Town Mayor. Some months later, in mid-September, he and young Megan-Leanne were wed. During their first year of marriage town life seemed uneventful enough. After the upheaval of the previous few years, this was to be welcomed. But when they'd been married about fifteen months, a letter arrived that disturbed them. The handwriting was barely legible, and it was obvious that the writer was not a man or woman of letters. Certainly, the hand was recognised by neither the Mayor nor his wife. The postmark revealed that it came from the Barony of Scarawalsh. On breaking the seal, it could readily be surmised that the letter had come from the pen of Amos Wickham. It seemed that Hendrick was ill, very ill, suffering from an affliction known as 'consumption'. The condition was irremediable. From what they could glean from Wickham's awful handwriting, Hendrick would survive for about another three months. Six at the most.

The Mayor and his wife immediately resolved to reconcile themselves to this wretched man while there was still time. As soon as Christmas was over and the days began to lengthen slightly, a chaise was arranged to take the couple the ten leagues up country to Newtownbarry. The Mayor and his wife intended to spend some four or five days in that place, making their peace with their former associate in his hermitical, misanthropic, condition. Alderman Parle would, as always, execute the duties of Mayor in Ferguson's absence, while Simon Lowney would assume temporary stewardship at the mill.

And so it was, in the spring of eighteen thirty-nine, that Mr. and Mrs. Robert Ferguson came to Newtownbarry in search of Michael Hendrick. The humble abode, which he and Amos Wickham had shared since they'd arrived two years before, was located at the top of the town. It was near to a bridge over the River Clody just at the boundary with County Carlow. When they pulled up outside the gate, they immediately recognised the figure that confronted them as Wickham himself. He looked deeply distressed and drew short breaths, as was his usual wont.

"Mister Hendrick's slippin' away fast," he began. "Y'ave to come and see him. See if yeh can get him to talk. He's barely respondin' to the doctor."

They all three entered the house directly. Upon catching their first glance of Hendrick it was immediately apparent to the Fergusons that their acquaintance had but hours to live, if not minutes.

"Might we be permitted a few moments in private?" asked Megan gently.

The doctor touched the brim of his hat to her and quietly departed the room. Wickham followed closing the door behind him. After several seconds of embarrassed silence, Megan looked at her husband imploringly.

"Ah, I see my dear," he said reading her intentions. "Privacy? You meant me too, didn't you?"

Megan, now with hands joined and eyes closed as if in prayer, nodded solemnly. Soon she and her stepfather were the only two present in the room. Death seemed to hang all around Hendrick's face. He looked gaunt, pale and shrivelled. But he remained conscious.

"Mr. Hendrick," whispered the girl. "It's me. It's Megan."

"What do yeh call me?" wheezed the dying man. "Yeh call me 'Mr. Hendrick'? After years o' callin' me yer father, I'm now nottin' more to yeh than the next man in the street."

"After years of *deception*, how can I call you anything else?" retorted the girl. Though her voice was gentle, her tone was one of reproof.

"Do yeh forgive me for Wellingtonbridge?" he pleaded, weakly moving his hand towards hers at the side of the bed.

"How can *I* forgive that incident, sir? *I* was not the party sinned against? You sold your wife and daughter a full year before I was even born. Your crime was not against your wife *or* your daughter. It was a heartless assault upon the family unit itself. You attacked the foundation of any Christian society. You undermined the very institution on which our civilisation is built, the family."

Megan Ferguson's extreme revulsion at any hint of impropriety was candidly obvious in this sermon to her dying stepfather. But Nature pays no tribute to such sensitivities in its readiness to disregard all social convention. The debacle at Wellingtonbridge, Susanna's gullibility in believing her union with the sailor to be morally binding, the death of an infant and the void that death created—this was the curious and improper chain of events out of which had sprung the most beautiful, respectable and sought-after maiden in County Wexford. She'd already remarked to her husband that he was, in fact, married to a bastard. But Robert had an answer for everything. Indeed he regarded the matter with some levity, and even comforted his wife by observing that Saint Joseph was descended from a prostitute.

"Then what o' my first deception?" continued the dying man, with much discomfort of both body and soul. "I was so afraid o' losin' yer love and devotion. Susanna was gone from us. I wanted to protect yeh, Megan. My pride was bigger than my love, I see that now. Curse my jealousy. Can't yeh still forgive me, and do it here at my own deathbed?"

"If only you'd have owned it to me at the time, sir," protested the young woman, tears welling in her eyes, "I might have learnt to love you, and loved you well. But to allow me go on for years in such ignorance of my own paternity?"

"I can't undo what happened at Wellingtonbridge. But I can still ask yeh to pray for me. I've not long to live. What a wretch I am."

Every sentence seemed to require more effort. Megan then promised to forgive him and they prayed together for a time.

"But what about my real father?" she sobbed. "When he came to Castlebridge, you sent him all the way back to Canada. I could have loved you both. But how could you be so heartless to that man? He was my *real* father and he came to Wexford to claim me and love me. Why all this deception? Was it really that bad?"

Megan could have talked and sobbed all day. Hendrick would never hear another word. He had slipped into a coma and the doctor was once again summoned.

"The cursed consumption's got the better of him alright," he said. "Not much more I can do."

Michael Hendrick lingered for a short time longer, then finally slipped away.

The morning after Hendrick's funeral, the Fergusons set about making their return journey to Castlebridge. Wickham, who had only moved to Newtownbarry on Hendrick's account, accompanied them and himself re-settled in the town of his birth. Their hearts were heavy as they trudged their way back across the county, and few words were spoken along the road.

Within weeks, life had essentially returned to normal at the Ferguson household. By now both husband and wife alike had learned how to put tragedy behind them as best any couple might. Naturally, certain days in the year were tinged with sadness, in particular the anniversaries of those who held a special place in their hearts. But they soldiered on. Ferguson was a popular Mayor and his business continued to thrive. Then, the following May, the couple announced the happy news of the birth of a healthy baby girl, whom they named Molly. That very summer, Ferguson was required to step down as Mayor having served for three terms. Johnny Parle, his deputy, would also stand down. The Corporation had unanimously elected Paddy Corish to succeed Ferguson to the Mayoralty, with Tommy Cavanagh as Deputy Mayor. Thus Ferguson found he could now devote time to the newly arrived daughter he so fondly cherished.

That September, the Ferguson family stunned Castlebridge by announcing their decision to remove to Kingstown—Robert's home town—and there to settle as a family. To honour Ferguson's outstanding contribution to the life of the neighbourhood, the Corporation laid on a lavish reception for the former Mayor at The South Leinster Arms. This was greatly attended and Mayor Corish paid a tribute to his predecessor that was both lengthy and flattering. Not a few tears were shed that night. Forty-eight hours later, the happy family departed from Castlebridge and set out on their twenty-five-league trek northwards.

Having sold up the barley business as well as Slaneyview House, the family found that they could afford to live comfortably by the sea. Their house was spacious, lavish and well located. It afforded a pleasant view of the coastline that stretched southwards from the Port of Kingstown to the quaint harbour at Sandycove. Robert, being well acquainted with its environs, succeeded in his commercial dealings in that place every bit as much as he had done in Wexford. What's more, his wife was warmly received by all his relatives and came to be regarded more as a sister than a sister-in-law.

As the years passed, another three baby girls graced the Ferguson household. Thus, Molly was soon joined by Susanna, then by Catherine and finally by the curly-haired Phoebe. Robert and Megan Ferguson were lovingly watchful of their children, and the family were a close-knit unit.

The extension of the railways to Wexford greatly lessened the inconvenience of travelling to and from that place. In fact, their living in close proximity to Kingstown station afforded the Fergusons every opportunity to visit the model county whenever they so desired. But such were expeditions of rare occurrence, and tended to occur chiefly in the summer months. The four girls would run wild on Curracloe beach while their parents reminisced about old times. In particular, the couple would fondly recall the day that Robert had made his proposal of marriage on those very sand dunes.

The Ferguson family enjoyed many happy years together. Megan and Robert derived immeasurable joy from witnessing their four daughters grow up and each make a relative success of her life. All four had been expensively educated and three had married into respectable families. By the turn of the century, Robert had passed away and his widow was growing old and infirm. Then at the age of eighty-nine, surrounded by four loving and devoted daughters as well as three committed sons-in-law, Megan-Leanne Ferguson finally drew her last breath. Three quarters of a century earlier, this most honest and sincere member of the human race had trusted that her Lord would go and prepare a place for her. It seemed that today was the day appointed to return and claim his treasure. Her daughters wept, blessed their mother's name, and comforted one another.

The funeral was more a celebration of a noble life than an occasion for great wailing and lamentation. It was agreed all over Kingstown that Megan-Leanne Ferguson was the most respectable, charitable, devoted and gentle matron that the town had ever known. These sentiments were echoed twenty-five leagues down the coast.

Despite the many disappointments of her younger days, this remarkable woman had stood firm throughout. What's more, her trials had not embittered her. She had not allowed them to. She had stoically resolved to prevent her spirit from ever descending into a state of perpetual regret, hankering after the distant past and wallowing in self-pity for the crosses her early life had thrust upon her. But the mature years of her life, those sixty-five or so spent in the household of Robert Ferguson, had vindicated her unshakable trust in the goodwill inherent in human nature, and in the God who had so infused our first parents with that most divine of all his attributes. Moreover, her experiences of this world (when contrasted with those of her stepfather) taught her that life, which can lavish innumerable blessings on those who reach out and seize it, is unrelentingly harsh upon those who have given up.

THE END

0-595-34414-3

Printed in the United Kingdom
by Lightning Source UK Ltd.
R320600001B/R3206PG103966UKSX00001B/1-9